ELECTRIC

ANGEL

a novel by

Sue Dent

Front cover and art design by Nicholas Grabowsky.
Front Cover image taken by professional photographer
Jim Sorfleet of SnS-photo
Cover model Gothic Illusionist and actor
Master Ron Fitzgerald.

Back cover design by Sue Dent
Back cover images of actor Dave Vescio with image
Provided by Jon Humphries of JonHumphries.Com
Permission given by Al "Mr. Outrageous" Burke
For the use of his image.

Edited by Arlene W. Robinson
Published by S D Enterprises

ISBN 978-0-9960121-8-8

For signings, personal appearances, or interviews, please contact Ms
Dent's publicist Matt Chassin at: Mattsmarketing.com

ELECTRIC ANGEL

AN S D ENTERPRISES Book - Ridgeland, Mississippi

Look for these S D Enterprises titles as well!

Never Ceese

Forever Richard

Cyn No More

Acknowledgements

I want to thank absolutely
Everyone for pushing me
To keep writing even
Though it seemed at times
that I would Never get enough
Attention to actually
Succeed. And by success
I mean being able to make a
Living for myself and my
Family by Doing something I love.
Like the lyrics from "Wake Me Up,"
by Avicii state, "I can't tell
where the journey will end, but I know
where to start." And I know who
I want to Travel with me along the way.
All of y'all!
I've said it before and I'll say it
Again. I couldn't do it without
Y'all and I wouldn't even try.
Enjoy!

Electric Angel

Sue Dent

Chapter 1

The two-lane road wound its way around the foothills of the lower Appalachians like a ribbon carelessly tossed on the ground. Anna Chadwick gripped the steering wheel tighter and eased her foot from the gas pedal. The long day's drive bearing down on her, she began to reconsider. *Nothing about this makes sense. No one just picks up and leaves everything behind. I don't even know where I'm headed.*

Panic took root. Confused tears blurred her vision. She wiped at them with the back of an uncertain hand, then gave her head a determined shake.

"No! You can do this. You *have* to do this." She placed a maternal hand on the small bulge of her stomach. "They deserve a chance. Both of them."

With this thought, she pushed away her panic and drove on. Yet when dusk threatened, the uneasy feeling returned. How much farther would she have to go? Was she on the right road? The landscape looked the same no matter which road she took, rolling hills populated by thick pockets of pines. With no directions, one could easily get lost in an area like this. She'd taken this road because at the moment she had to make a decision, it seemed the road to take.

Now, she wasn't sure. Nothing really distinguished this road from the other five or six she passed up already. That suffocating thought was enough to make her consider turning around.

Then, as the road curved, she saw it.

"Yes," she sighed. Just like the dream, the recurring dream that began over a month ago, one that had her driving this very road. *Yes, this road,* she thought, and nodded, all doubt gone. *I remember this. I remember all of this. There's the weathered old billboard. That barn too!* She drove the car to the top of the next hill. "And that!"

She jerked the steering wheel hard and pressed on the brakes; the car skidded onto the shoulder. The instant the vehicle screeched to a stop, she shoved the gearshift into park, pressed the button to lower the driver's-side window and stared out. "I'm not crazy," she half-laughed and cried. "I'm not!"

She studied the quaint one-level motel with a keen eye that confirmed it appeared exactly as it did in last night's dream, the only time she'd seen anything in the dream other than the road itself and surrounding landscape. She looked up at the unlit neon sign, also new to last night's dream, and read aloud, "Mountain View Inn."

She gave herself a moment, just a moment to recover, then shifted the car back into drive, pulled into the motel's parking lot and stopped under the office's covered awning. Loose gravel crunched beneath her feet when she stepped out, and the unlit neon sign popped and buzzed to life in the sultry dusk alive with the sounds of cicadas.

* * *

Mountain View Inn belonged to recently widowed Martha Keltz. Following the death of her husband, she took up residence at the inn. She wasn't much on driving, and home before her husband passed was a thirty-minute trip at best.

The winter months at Mountain View were the busy months. Few customers stopped by any other time of the year. Therefore Martha took her time when she heard the small copper bell over the door clatter loudly. Frumpishly dressed and not overly excited about being interrupted, she turned the volume down on her game show, pushed herself up from her recliner and lumbered out of her office/apartment. *More than likely just someone needing directions*, she thought.

She glanced at the young woman on the other side of the counter. She looked to be in her mid to late twenties, maybe early thirties. Something about her made it hard to tell. Martha wrote it off as just someone who appeared older than their actual age. But this individual also looked tired.

"Can I help you?" she asked. Something else told her she wanted more than directions.

"I'd like a room for the evening."

Martha didn't make a habit of turning customers down but in the off-season she often did. If enough daylight remained, she always encouraged potential customers to drive on. She only made exceptions if more than one room would be needed. "You might do better driving on a bit farther. I don't usually get a lot of business this time of year. And there aren't any restaurants or shops around either. Plenty more accommodations if you drive a little further north."

The young woman replied, "So you don't have any vacancies?"

"Goodness yes I have vacancies. I just wanted to let you know you'd have more to choose from if you continued on

3

north a little ways. As you can see, there isn't much around here."

Her guest breathed relief. "I'd prefer not to drive on."

"All right." Martha shrugged, looked past her customer to her car parked outside. "You're traveling alone?"

"Yes."

"Then I'll put you close to the office." She pulled out a ledger to begin the check-in process.

"I'd like to be as far away from the office as possible. If you don't mind."

Martha looked up, confused. "You're traveling alone, and you'd like a room away from the office?"

"Yes."

The young woman seemed certain enough, but Martha wasn't. Why would a young woman traveling alone want to stay at the other end of the motel, when she could choose from any other room? No real reason came, so she took a stab at it. "I don't make that much noise if that's your concern."

Her customer shifted uneasily. "I just really prefer to have the room I asked for."

Martha went back to her ledger shaking her head. It wasn't like the room wasn't ready for a guest. "Suit yourself. I'll put you at the very end, then. And oh, my name is Martha…."

* * *

Anna dug into her purse and handed Martha a credit card and her license, relieved she'd finally convinced the innkeeper that she was certain of her decision. She didn't know how much longer she could hold up under the scrutiny. She wasn't prepared to explain why she didn't want to drive on.

4

Martha grabbed at a pair of reading glasses that hung around her neck and set them in place on the end of her nose. Just as she leaned down to write, the door behind her, left ajar when she exited, opened a little farther. Curious, Anna glanced that way but saw nothing to explain the door opening as far as it did, too much for a draft to have moved it.

She had her answer when an energetic Pomeranian came bounding around the desk, its tiny nails clacking about on the tile floor. "Well aren't you just the cutest thing," she said.

Martha glanced over her shoulder at the slightly opened door. "I guess I didn't pull that shut when I came out." She peered over the counter, over the top of her glasses. "Some guests don't mind her. Others do. Plus I never know how Mimi will react."

Anna knelt down to pet the small dog. "But she's so sweet."

"Most of the time, but I can't take a chance. She *is* good company though. And she's a good judge of character. She seems to like you."

Anna straightened when she looked up and saw Martha with her key. Mimi took her enthusiasm back to the other side of the desk, where a treat awaited her.

"Just sign here and we're done." Martha leaned forward slightly. "If you change your mind ... about wanting a closer room I mean ... just let me know."

Chapter 2

Anna declined Martha's offer to show her to her room. She was ready to be alone. She drove her car around to the room on the end and parked, gathered her purse, pulled the straps over one shoulder, and collected the one overnight bag she'd packed that morning. She then straightened and inhaled deep. The thick musk of pine worked to relax her, as did the collective mating drone of male cicadas' that rose and fell with fervor.

A moment later she locked her car, took her room key in hand and noticed as she walked that the sun had disappeared behind the thick ridge of pines to the west. The weight of her journey crashed down on her. She was truly tired.

She unlocked the room's door and stepped inside. Two lamps atop matching tables flanked the bed, and came on when she flipped a switch beside her. The light they offered was dim, but enough to make out the modestly decorated room: a king-size bed, a long desk along the wall adjacent to it. She walked over to the dresser's mirror and stared at her reflection, confirmed she indeed looked as tired as she felt.

"Boo," she said to her waiflike image. "Aren't you a sight?"

She pushed back a lock of pale blonde hair, shivered when she saw several individual strands break off and fall at her touch. Her hair used to be something she was proud of.

Turning away from the mirror, she pulled her arms around her tight. According to the thermostat on the wall, it was a comfortable seventy-five degrees yet she felt cold.

She knew her weight had a lot to do with that. She'd dropped five pounds in just the last month. Where once she'd been a fit 120 pounds, the scale this morning barely registered 110. So much about her had changed. It didn't bother her though. How could it? By all accounts, she should be dead. And she would've been, if not for the visitor that night at the hospital, a visit Anna deemed as divine intervention since nothing else made sense.

And divine intervention made perfect sense, since she'd prayed that somehow her unborn children be spared the untimely death sentence handed to her. She accepted she was dying, yet she didn't want that for her children. She wanted them to have a chance. Shortly after that prayer went out, the visitor—the entity— came to call. Seconds before the heart monitor flat-lined, she heard it—or felt it, she still wasn't sure. It came to her and gave her this message: *I can help you Anna Chadwick. I can save your children if you allow it.*

No matter how hard she tried to get the doctors to tell her otherwise, none could tell her that her children could be saved. And now this voice did. The following morning, after conditions took a dramatic turn for the better, those same doctors, stunned by her miraculous recovery, couldn't keep her from going home with at least another month to live.

7

Anna placed her purse on the bed and reached inside it for the prenatal vitamins she'd packed earlier. Her doctor only prescribed them at her insistence. He saw no real benefit, and tried to explain that to her. But the doctor didn't know what she knew, and since prescribing the vitamins didn't actually hurt anything, he humored her.

Vitamins in hand, she walked to the sink and picked up a glass and removed the protective shrink-wrap, then drew water from the tap and used the water to down the vitamins. She laughed at the fluttering in her womb, so much like a startled butterfly flitting about, just like she'd heard. "I'll bet you two were thirsty." She said "you two" even though the ultrasound confirmed one twin would be stillborn. The visitor said she could save both children though and this is what Anna chose to believe.

After the day's drive, it felt good to just stretch out, as she did now on the king-size bed. Her purse was next to her; she pulled it over and reached inside for the pamphlets. The images on each one varied, but all of them had some artist's depiction of her disease. She opened the first one and reread the words partly responsible for her journey today.

Women diagnosed with Acute Lymphoblastic Leukemia who decline both termination and chemotherapy often die with the previable fetus in utero.

If only things had happened differently. If only she could've known about the cancer before she and Zachary decided to start a family.

"Zachary," she said, not realizing she was speaking aloud or whimpering her husband's name. She'd kept everything a secret. She hadn't explained about the entity or anything else. Yet how could she explain what she didn't understand herself?

The deep sting of guilt shot through her, recalling the short note she'd left that morning, to say she would return after she worked things out. Zachary deserved better. But if things went as the entity promised, she wouldn't have to explain anything. She could just return home and Zachary would be overjoyed to see her. Even though it wouldn't be her.

* * *

At the piercing high-pitched beep, Martha flailed about in her recliner, roused from her doze. A lightning flash outside had Mimi up and barking and frantically running in concentric arcs around the recliner. The weather radio sat on the table next to the recliner. She stabbed the button to silence it, then took hold of the television remote.

The show she'd been watching wasn't on the screen. Instead it was the local weatherman, talking about intense storms moving through the area.

"Come on, Mimi," Martha said while she pushed herself up and out of the chair. "Let's get you one of your pills before it gets worse." As she often did, she wondered if Mimi's terror of storms and lightning had to do with the electrical discharge, thinking that a dog's senses might be affected somehow.

On her way across the room, she stopped to peer out the window that faced the parking lot. Her guest hadn't

9

changed her mind. Martha sighed deeply and moved along to her kitchen. "It just doesn't make sense," she muttered. "A young woman traveling alone should be smarter. And now there's a storm coming."

Another flash of lightning, another flare-up by Mimi, and she moved on to get the medicine.

Chapter 3

Anna lay on her side, the additional weight in her abdomen making this position more comfortable than lying on her back, her preference when resting. Until just a few weeks ago it hadn't really mattered, now it did. At the thought of how quickly the pregnancy had progressed, a silent tear slid down her cheek.

It had been three days since she'd last taken the medication her doctor prescribed. Now, there was nothing to slow the cancer. After she left the hospital that day, after her short-lived recovery, the doctors insisted she continue taking the medication. But the medication had warnings for pregnant women and she didn't want to take any more chances. Yet three days with no medicine meant it wouldn't be long. She went to wipe the tear away from her cheek but realized she couldn't even raise her arm. *Weak, so weak.* She'd prayed that night in the hospital. She prayed again now. Another plea for the two lives she carried: *Save my babies.* A silent plea. She tried to say the words aloud, but had no energy or strength.

* * *

It hovered in the atmosphere just above earth, and pulsated in rhythm with Anna's weakening heartbeat, absorbing and ingesting energy from spiraling filaments of

11

plasma. It pulsated slower as Anna's heart did, then began to descend toward earth. It traveled a planned path, a destination in mind while it moved with purpose and direction as though heading toward a beacon. It easily navigated through the first few layers of earth's atmosphere before it ran into trouble.

The storm clouds extended some forty thousand feet into the atmosphere. Negative and positively charged molecules within the clouds combined and discharged. Each discharge disoriented and confused the entity off its planned path. It struggled to stay on course.

* * *

The vet had said to give her one tablet, but then told Martha to use her discretion. Mimi had reacted so horribly to the lightning, so much worse than usual, if that were even possible, Martha did give Mimi two of the pills. Her pet settled almost instantly. As the lightning continued outside, Martha was glad she'd doubled the dose.

The cloud-to-cloud lightning continued to illuminate the night sky outside, but according to the weatherman, the worst of the storms had passed to the south. Perhaps she could get some sleep now as well. She reached to pull the blinds shut when a brilliant bolt shot from the sky. She threw an arm up over her eyes to protect against the sheer brightness; when she lowered it, her mouth fell open. The bolt had hit the large neon sign out front. Colored neon gas exploded out of the tubes that carried it. The plastic parts of the sign had shredded and were raining down. Mouth agape, she stood and stared at the empty metal frame. She could just make it out as the lightning continued to flash.

* * *

At first, Anna couldn't tell what had changed her limbo-like state, just that something had.

With renewed energy from what seemed like a short nap, she pushed up on her elbows, breathed in as someone who'd been drowning and had just broken the water's surface. She took a moment to settle then realized, with no one in sight, she didn't feel alone anymore. The hairs on her arms and the back of her neck stood on end. This sensation, she recognized from that night in the hospital.

Static electricity, she thought. *It's here.*

Yes. Just as I promised.

Anna heard no voice but the words were clear in her mind. While she was trying to form an answer, the entity spoke again.

But I'm afraid my arrival might have caused some structural damage. The sign I used as a beacon exploded upon impact.

She gasped concern. "You weren't hurt?"

Just a little disoriented by the large discharges of electricity from the storm.

Anna's thoughts went immediately to the life this entity carried, but before she could ask the entity answered, *We're both fine.*

Anna no longer had the energy to hold herself up on her elbows, and lowered herself to the pillow. "I'm so weak. I know the time is close."

It is.

"I ... I can't tell you how much this means to me."

I have trouble expressing the enormity of my gratitude as well. Without you, the life I carry would have no chance at all.

"It seems God knows what he's doing," Anna whispered. "I prayed, you know ... for my children to be spared."

As did I.

13

So prayer is universal, Anna thought. *Or rather, galactic.* This supported her theory of divine intervention. Then, she remembered: When they'd done the ultrasound, they only found one heartbeat. Anna was told one twin would either be absorbed by her body, or be stillborn. She closed her eyes, breathed deep. "And ... what you said before ... you can save both children?"

My offspring will play host to your son's body. Give it life in the same manner I will do for you. In fact, this is already happening.

"I don't feel any differ—" Something kicked inside her. She managed a little laugh. Oh my, I felt that."

Would you like to visit with them before you leave? Would you like to visit with the boys?

"Boys? You can tell?" It had been too early at the time of the ultrasound. "Yes. I'd love to see them. Can I see them now?"

Whenever you're ready Anna Chadwick.

"Please, call me Anna. Do you have a name?"

I do not carry a label as such.

"Well, I have to call you something. Even angels have names, and you're certainly that." She mused over her options. "How about I just refer to you as my electric angel? That certainly fits you."

Very well Anna. And if you are ready now, I believe I can facilitate the visit.

She gazed around the room and closed her eyes. "I am ready."

* * *

"Yes. Hello. I'm not sure who I should speak to—never had to call 911 before about something like this. But I need to report storm damage. Lightning just struck the big sign in front of my motel. Yes, Mountain View Inn. The damn thing just exploded! There's plastic and glass everywhere. I just wanted to let someone know. There might be debris in the road."

Martha listened while the voice on the other end asked questions. "Yes," she said. "We still have power, though the lights do keep dimming. Like the load is too much." She looked up as the lights dimmed and brightened once more, then returned to a steady glow. "Never mind," she said after a moment. "That problem seems to have straightened itself out. But I am worried someone will drive over something broken and lose a tire or something. Yes … thank you."

She hung up and went back to the window, then thought of her shy guest. She hadn't heard a peep out of her. She glanced at the telephone, wondered if she should try her room, just in case she was huddled in there, frightened about the noise. *But why?* she finally decided. If the exploding sign hadn't bothered her enough to call the office then she must be fine.

Chapter 4

The cicadas no longer droned. The storm had passed. It was seven-thirty the following morning. Anna's form lay motionless on the bed. The only visible sign she still lived was the subtle rise and fall of her chest. Then her eyes fluttered open.

After a moment, she pushed herself up, swung her legs over the edge and sat. She took the prenatal vitamins from her purse, still next to her on the bed, and washed two down with a glass of water. She did all of this just as if everything was the same.

* * *

Feather duster in hand, Martha straightened and turned toward the lobby's front door when the brass bell over it clanged. "Good morning," she said to her only guest, indicated a tray of breakfast rolls under a domed Plexiglas cover. "I put some sweet rolls out if you want some. Made a fresh pot of coffee too. That was quite a storm we had last night. Did you sleep well?"

Anna opened her mouth but no words came out. At least not right away. A good minute passed before finally she replied, "I ... slept well. Thank you."

"Okay," Martha replied, though baffled by why it took Anna so long to answer a simple question. "I guess you've come to check out, then."

"Yes."

At least that answer came without delay.

Martha moved over to take the room key Anna proffered, but stopped short when Mimi raced out from behind the counter, barking and yapping as if the storm last night were in full swing again. And her aggression seemed to be aimed at Anna.

"I don't understand," Martha said while she bent to scoop Mimi up with one arm. "She warmed up so fast to you yesterday. Perhaps it's the medicine I gave her last night. Something the vet prescribed for her. She's terrified of storms." She gave an embarrassed chuckle. "Mimi's terrified, not the vet."

Eyes wide, Mimi continued to emit low growls. Martha apologetically reached out with her free hand to take the key Anna held out. "I'm so very sorry she's acting this way. You're all paid up, so I'll just take that so you can be on your way—"

When she grabbed onto the jagged metal end, her body tensed and stiffened, and low gurgling sounds came from her throat. She remained like that until Anna yanked the key away.

"I—I'm sorry," Anna stammered, backed away and placed the key on the check-in desk instead. "I haven't quite adjusted yet. I'm truly sorry."

The bell over the door clanged upon her exit. Breathing hard, Martha tilted her head down to look at Mimi cradled in the nook of her arm. Every golden hair on Mimi's body stood on end, or so it seemed. Martha then caught sight of her own image in a nearby mirror; her mousy brown hair formed a bizarre halo around her head. "Would you look at that," she whispered. "Would you just look at that."

* * *

The offices of Anderson Electric took up the top five floors of a twenty-story office building in the heart of downtown Newark. Under the driven leadership of Fritz Anderson, the family-based company had grown substantially. Not only did the company provide power to rural New Jersey, but also parts of New York, swallowing up several local competitors in the process.

Reginald Palmer, head of personnel and the only employee Fritz Anderson didn't oust when he took the company over, began to organize the papers spread out before him on the conference table. The last department head had just reported. Each of the seven, gathered on either side of the long mahogany table, now sat in anxious limbo.

Fritz, at the head of the table and framed by a huge window behind him, stared over steepled fingers like a hawk considering its prey. Of Mediterranean descent, his aquiline nose with prominent bridge gave substance to his heritage, as did his dark, deep-set eyes. Fritz, notorious for firing at least one employee at the end of each monthly meeting, glared at each one in turn. The mood was aptly tense.

"Meeting adjourned," he quipped as though they'd all been lucky that he wasn't in a worse mood. "You're dismissed."

Pie charts, computer-generated graphs and financial reports were gathered together. Briefcases stuffed.

"Except for you."

The room grew ominously quiet until the seven preparing to leave realized they weren't the one who'd been asked to remain.

Reginald Palmer, half-standing and half-sitting, sank back into his seat.

18

"Not there," Fritz motioned. "Here." He indicated the chair closest him at the end of the table. As the others filed out, their faces those of hostages who'd just been released from their captors, Reg gathered up his papers and moved. At the sound of the conference room door shutting, Fritz grinned. "Let's do lunch today, Reg. How about the Mayflower?"

Reg rolled his eyes. "You enjoy doing that don't you? You do realize they're all going to think I got the ax."

"They know better, or at least they should. So what do you say about lunch?"

"Sure." Reg straightened his notes from the meeting again. Unlatched and opened his briefcase. "Lunch is fine." He latched the case a final time, then moved to get up. "Just let me go check on a few—"

Fritz grabbed Reg by an arm. "Wait. I actually did have something else on my mind too."

Reg glanced at the hand Fritz had clutched his arm with, then looked back at Fritz. "Okay, what is it?"

"It's about our man Zachary."

Reg sighed. "I know. He's been a bit preoccupied lately."

"Lately, and for quite a few months. Long weekends, leaving work early, pushing to use vacation days he hasn't even accrued yet. That's more than preoccupied."

"I'm not saying you don't have a right to be concerned—"

"Good."

"But his wife is dying of cancer."

"Don't feed me that crap, Reg. I've been very lenient with Zachary, but he's not the only employee with problems and you know it. Remember when Johnson lost his wife and kids two years ago when their SUV hit a patch

19

of ice on that mountain? He was back at work two weeks later. Didn't skip a beat. Death is a part of life, but so is living. And working." Fritz's face lightened a bit. "Look, Zachary's done some great work on the Smart Grid Project, just as you promised he would. He's put us ahead of the game in many ways. But with all his absence? Gives the competition a chance to catch up, and I've worked too long and hard to let that happen. I need him here, Reg."

"Yeah," Reg replied. Agreeing with Fritz came with the job. "I'll see what I can do."

Fritz clutched Reg's right shoulder, offered a conciliatory smile to make up for being so demanding. "I knew I could count on you."

* * *

Reg left work early with Fritz's request, that wasn't really a request, heavy on his mind. Oh, he'd talked to other employees before in similar situations. But Zachary was a friend as well. A close friend. As children, they lived in the same neighborhood. On the same street. They attended the same high school and hung out with the same group of friends. They cut class together and during their rebellious years, even smoked pot together on rare occasions when they could pull together enough cash to risk it.

After high school Reg went to college nearby. Zachary headed off to MIT to take advantage of a full scholarship he'd earned. What a surprise that their paths would cross again fourteen years later, with Zachary's name being first on a shortlist of candidates provided by the headhunter recruiter Reg had solicited.

"Yes, it's a big fee to pay," Reg explained to Fritz, "but Zachary's worth it. And you wanted someone with smart grid experience. Zachary's pretty much the go-to man for that."

20

Fritz gave the okay to hire Zachary the following day.

Reg pulled up to the security gate at the neighborhood's entrance, lowered his window and reached out his arm to key in the visitor's code. He waited for the gate to open, then drove on. *When will the words come?* he thought. This wasn't going to be easy.

Zachary's house sat on an acre of well-manicured lawn. Clippings from the recently mowed yard sat on the curb in appropriately marked bags. For a fee, the neighborhood association provided lawn service. Strategically aimed sprinklers watered what needed watering.

Reg parked in front of the house, just past the fresh lawn clippings. He didn't want to be in the way if someone needed to leave via the driveway. He grabbed his briefcase from the seat beside him and followed the sidewalk around to the front door, had raised his hand to knock when the door was jerked open. With eyes clearly in need of sleep, Zachary stared out. He still wore the clothes he'd had on yesterday at work, a polo shirt with khakis. Wednesday was casual day. Today was Thursday. The shirt was no longer tucked in, the pants slightly wrinkled. His reddish-brown hair showed grooves where fingers had recently plowed through. Reg thought out loud, "You've been up all night."

Zachary stood five-foot eight to Reg's five-six yet with shoulders slumped and head drooped forward, he appeared much shorter. "I thought you were Anna."

Zachary didn't even bother to invite Reg in. Just walked off into the house. Reg closed the front door and followed him. "She not here?" Reg said to his back.

Zachary sank into a chair. A lamp lit the tabletop beside it. A cell phone lay charging. He picked up a piece of paper and held it out. Reg took the note and read it. "So how long has she been gone?"

21

"I found the note after I got home from work yesterday."

"That's why you didn't come in this morning," Reg said. "Did you call the police?"

"They won't do anything. She's not been gone long enough. And since she left a note—"

"Right," Reg nodded.   "You've no idea where she went?"

"None at all."

Zachary broke the brief silence that followed. "Why are you here? Shouldn't you be at work?"

"I came to check on you."

Zachary didn't seem to buy that. "Fritz sent you, didn't he?"

"No. But he *is* becoming frustrated, and I'm running out of ways to humor him."

"I should just quit. So he can find someone else and move on."

Reg moved to the edge of the couch, and with all the skills of a master strategist, prepared to try to get through to Zachary. If he quit he'd lose more than his job. He'd owe Fritz money and a lot of it. He'd have to reimburse Anderson Electric the headhunter's fee if he left the company before the predetermined time. Reg knew Zachary wasn't thinking about this. "No, you shouldn't quit," he said. "And no one else can do the job Fritz hired you to do. Come on Zachary, you're not thinking clearly. Don't make rash decisions. Anna will be back soon, and you'll be fine."

Zachary's eyes rounded at a sudden mechanical droning and he shot to his feet. "It's the garage door," he mumbled over his shoulder as he raced toward the kitchen. Reg followed, and saw him heading toward the door he knew led to the garage.

Chapter 5

The garage door closed as Anna stepped from the car, and Zachary tried not to grab her too hard as he embraced her, then held her at arm's length. "My God Anna, where've you been?" His voice trembled in his relief. "I was worried sick about you."

"I'm fine, Zachary."

But was she? Something about her—something was different. It seemed a good difference, but he couldn't quite figure out what it was. Then, he realized. "You— you look ... great. I mean, you look rested. Livelier. And your eyes. I've always loved them, but ... they're beautiful. Since you've been sick ... it's like they're still blue, but they're *sparkling* blue now."

"I know," she said with a smile. "And I wanted to tell you—" She stopped. Put a hand to her abdomen. "Oh my."

He put a hand out to steady her. "What is it? Is something wrong?" She looked so well now. Was she going to relapse right there in front of him?

She took his other hand and placed it on her stomach. Held it there for a good three seconds. "Did you feel that?"

His mouth formed an O. "I—I did. It kicked."

"He kicked."

"Really? A boy?" Then it hit him. "Is that where you went? To get another ultrasound?"

"Sort of. But let's talk about it inside."

"Of course."

Reg stood just inside the doorway that led into the kitchen. "The baby," Zachary said, eager to share, "it's a boy. That's where Anna has been … to get an ultrasound." He stalled when he realized he had no more information than that. "At least that's part of it."

Reg stared at Anna. "I thought the doctor said you'd not be able to carry either child to term."

"Things are different now," Anna replied. "There's this new drug therapy. I didn't tell Zachary because I didn't want him to get his hopes up in case things didn't work out."

"What doctor did you go see?"

"You wouldn't know him."

"I might. Try me."

Instead of answering, Anna turned to Zachary. "I'd really like to talk to you about things first."

"Of course," Zachary replied. "I'm sure Reg understands. Don't you, Reg?"

For a moment their eyes locked, but Reg succumbed "Sure. I have to be going anyway. Anna," he faced her once more. "I'm glad you're back and safe. And Zachary, I'll see you at work tomorrow?"

Zachary turned to Anna. How he responded would depend on if she needed him.

Anna answered for him. "He'll be there."

* * *

Reg made the quickest getaway he could without appearing rude, and told them he'd see himself out. He stopped on the stoop and turned back toward the door he'd just pulled shut. The feeling that there was something different about Anna wouldn't leave him. And why didn't

24

Zachary push her to answer the question about the new drug therapy and this new doctor?

As he put his key in the ignition, Reg shook his head. He hadn't known Anna as long as he'd known Reg. Yet she seemed like an honest person with good intentions. What little he did know about her, he'd learned from Zachary. An only child of an older couple surprised by her conception since they were told they couldn't have children, Anna grew up extraordinarily protected. Both parents had passed by the time Zachary met her. To the best of his knowledge, Anna had made no real friends since she and Zachary had moved to the suburbs of Newark, and she'd politely turned down any effort he made to introduce her to some of the other wives.

But then why should any of that matter to him? If Anna could get Zachary to work in the morning, it was none of his business what he did or didn't know about her or what that something different was that had him wondering. Fritz would be calmed, Zachary would still have a job, and he could get back to running the personnel office again.

He put the car in drive, pulled away from the curb and headed home.

* * *

At the sound of the front door closing, Anna turned to Zachary. "You really should've gone into work," she said gently. Having full access to memories, the entity now known as Anna figured this out easily and deduced right away that Zachary needed to keep his job for things to go smoothly. "You've missed so many days."

"You were gone, Anna. And I didn't know where you were. All I had was that note. I tried to call your cell but you wouldn't answer. I called quite a few times."

25

She looked away, searched memories for a look she knew he'd respond to, then turned back to face him. "I know," she said, head slightly tilted to one side. Not making eye contact seemed important too. "I just didn't want to talk to you until I had good news."

The look worked. Zachary rushed the two steps over and pulled her to him. "Please don't be upset, honey. I didn't mean to make you feel bad. I just—I was just worried, that's all."

She allowed him to comfort her, then eased away. "Well, it is good news, isn't it? To learn I'll be able to carry the baby to term."

"Of course. That's wonderful news. But what about you? And what's this new therapy? How much longer will it give you?"

She made her eyes smile. "That's something else I'd like to talk to you about."

* * *

Waiting for the five-o'clock traffic to start moving again, Reg sat with his cell phone pressed to his ear. When Fritz answered he said, "Zachary will be at work tomorrow."

"Wonderful," Fritz replied. "And what about from now on?"

"If I thought there'd be a problem I would've told you that first." Reg didn't care if he sounded annoyed. Zachary was a friend, and when it came to business, Fritz put so little stock in such things.

"Good job, Reg," Fritz said after a pause. "I knew I could count on you."

The words didn't make Reg feel as though he'd done a good job. He'd simply done what he must, to keep bad things from happening to his friend. Lunch that day had amounted to Fritz outlining actions that would be taken if Zachary didn't start showing up for work. Thanks to Zachary's contract, Fritz couldn't make a move. Zachary hadn't done anything to warrant being let go. But Reg knew Fritz had ways.

"So he's off the fast track for a quick removal," Reg said now. "You'll call off your dogs."

"I'm sorry, I don't know what you're talking about," Fritz replied, a sudden coldness to his tone.

Reg decided it would be best to leave things at that. "Just know that Zachary will be at work tomorrow."

They ended the call when traffic started moving again. Reg wasn't a drinker, but tonight seemed to call for a scotch, or maybe two.

Chapter 6

With Reg gone, Anna opened up. Zachary was finding each sentence more interesting than the one before. Or maybe the right word was frustrating. Either way, every answer she gave him seemed to only make him want more.

"Something else?" he repeated. For the first time in months, Anna had news she seemed happy about sharing. There'd been nothing but bad news since the onset of the cancer, with the exception of the short-lived recovery that night in the hospital about a month ago. "So tell me. Whatever it is, I want to know."

"I'm not your Anna."

He was stuck between happy, and confused. He waited for her to clarify. When she didn't give him any more to go on, he said, "That's it? That's what you wanted tell me?"

"Yes. I'm not your Anna. Your Anna is gone."

"I don't understand. What do you—?"

She pointed her finger toward the counter behind him. He whipped his head around in time to see sparks coming from the toaster, a mini-fireworks show. Fire shot from the outlet, then sputtered out.

"I'm not your Anna," she repeated.

He swiveled his head back to look at her. Something in his eyes must have told her he wasn't convinced; she pointed again. He turned his head in time to see sparks shoot from the blender. A bluish flash licked at the plastic cover of the wall outlet and left it blackened upon retreat. He'd been too shocked the first time, but he made a valiant effort to save the blender. By the time he got to where it was, it had already met its demise. With wispy white electrical smoke still swirling, he turned and said, his voice thick, "So if you're not Anna, then what the hell are you?"

"Since, like you, I have a soul," she said, "it isn't accurate to ask what I am, but rather who."

He conceded, to save the rest of the small appliances in the house as well as his sanity. He couldn't deny it was Anna's voice he was hearing. But the words? She seemed to be practicing lines for a performance he knew nothing about.

"Anna," he pleaded, "why don't we just call your doctor and let him know what's going on? We'll tell him you're not quite yourself."

"But I am quite myself," she replied. "Even though getting used to this form is very much of a challenge." She held her hands out in front of her. Studied them as though looking for defects in her costume.

She's delusional, that's it, Zachary thought. Taking advantage of her being distracted, he darted for the phone on the wall. Snatched the receiver up and stabbed at the buttons. Anna whipped her head around. Pointed directly at him.

The jolt caused his body to convulse and jerk about. When she dropped her hand to her side, he collapsed. Fell to the floor like a limp ragdoll. He heard her gasp. Felt her gently lay her hand on his shoulder.

29

"I'm sorry," she said, sounding much like the Anna he knew and loved. *A dream*, he thought. *It's a bad dream, and now I'm going to wake up*

"But I can't let you call anyone. They wouldn't understand."

He let his head drop back to the floor. *No dream. Still the same nightmare.* Disillusioned and discouraged, he spoke, his words a mere breath of air. "At least if you let me call—I wouldn't be alone about not understanding."

Seconds later he felt a tingling sensation, not nearly as powerful as the jolt from a moment ago, and heard her say, "This should help you understand. This should comfort you."

The sensation coaxed him into a dreamlike slumber where he saw her—he saw Anna. She stood near the island-counter as she spoke. "I know how confusing this must be to you."

Standing, he turned to face her. He knew this voice. Nothing about it seemed contrived or different.

"I thought you might need me to explain—"

He rushed to embrace her but his arms flailed through the form that wasn't there. He backed up a step, glanced over his shoulder. Spotted his form and the form of the other Anna lying on the kitchen floor. Of course he was dreaming.

"You're not dreaming. I'm a memory. I've already passed. I left this memory to help you understand. I need you to understand so our children can survive."

"Children? But I thought the doctors said—"

"I know what the doctors said but their expertise is limited. They did the best they could." Anna nodded toward the figure on the floor. "She's already working to save both children."

30

He glanced over his shoulder to Anna's form lying next to his on the kitchen floor. "So that isn't you?"

"No, but you'll need to pretend that she is."

He swung his head back around to face her. "I won't. How could I ever? If she isn't you, I can't possibly pretend she is—"

"She carries your son, Zachary. Our son. You have to help her. You know how much it meant to both of us to have a child, and then the cancer came. Please Zachary. He's a part of me. Don't let him die…."

Unsure how much time had passed, he pushed open his heavy eyelids. Faced Anna's form and knew right away he was no longer dreaming. He pushed himself up, struggled to come to terms with what he'd just witnessed, and more importantly, how he now felt. Anna had just spoken to him. *His* Anna. It wasn't a dream. It was real.

"I'll help," he said to the unconscious form, carefully reaching under her. "I'll do whatever you need me to do. For Anna … for our son."

Her arms dangled when he lifted. Her head rested against his chest. He moved at a steady pace across the living room then carefully up the stairs until he came to the master bedroom. He eased her onto the bed before heading back downstairs. The entity had been specific about what it needed to survive, laid it all out moments before he came to. He now headed off to get the things he'd need.

At the bottom of the stairs he took a right toward the kitchen, went to the silverware drawer and selected two wide-bladed butter knives, then headed to the garage. From a plastic bin he grabbed two big rolls of electrical tape. On his way back in, he stopped to pull a rolled-up power cord from its hook near the back door and hefted it onto his shoulder.

31

Back upstairs, he settled on the opposite side of the bed, then spread out the items he'd carried up with him, his back to Anna. He leaned a bit to the side, slid a hand in a front pants pocket and came out with the pocketknife he kept there. With it he sliced off the adapter end of the utility cord, then continued to use the knife to score its protective rubber sheathing. With two wires exposed and bared, he took one of the butter knives in hand but then paused, not in indecision, but to make sure the process he was about to use was correct and logical. It was. He taped one bare wire to the knife with electrical tape, and continued to wrap the handle to ensure good insulation.

He repeated the procedure with the second wire and second butter knife. Once finished, he stood, pushed the utility cord back up onto his shoulder and walked around the bed. With a knee, he shoved a side table away from the wall to get to the outlet behind it. Holding the knives by their taped handles, careful not to let them touch, he leaned down and cautiously plugged the utility cord in. Both knives now carried a full electrical charge.

Standing over Anna, Zachary wondered about the instructions. *What if I misunderstood?* This big an electrical jolt could kill a human. An urgency swept over him and he pushed his doubt aside. He had to act now or it would be too late. He drew a determined breath, then laid a charged knife blade on either side of Anna's neck.

* * *

Reg went in to work early the following morning, earlier than usual anyway. Six-fifteen found him at his desk catching up on emails. Leaving work early the day before meant he had plenty to sort through. By seven, he'd successfully cleared most of the messages and relegated those not requiring an immediate response to a folder he'd look at later. Then he took up his empty cup and headed to get more coffee.

At the place where the two hallways intersected, he stopped. Zachary wasn't due in until eight, yet there was light under his door. He rapped, hesitant, then stuck his head in. Zachary bolted from around the desk like a racehorse charging the gate, pulled Reg the rest of the way in and shut the door behind him.

"Well I'm glad to see you too," Reg said, glanced at the watch on his wrist, "and early at that."

"I've got something to tell you," Zachary said. "Something you're not going to believe. Something about Anna. Sort of. But it's not really Anna—"

"No," Reg blurted, his heart registering an unreasonable amount of alarm: unreasonable, since he had no way of knowing what Zachary wanted to tell him, but he suspected whatever it was would sound crazy. "I mean n—not here. Not now. I'm on my way to a meeting. But you can tell me at lunch. All right? We'll do lunch."

Looking deflated for only a second, Zachary nodded. "Do you want me to come by your office?"

"No. I'll swing by and get you."

Reg stopped by his office long enough to slam his empty cup down on his desk. His agitation seemed to grow with each step he took toward Fritz Anderson's office. He pushed the closed door open, strode in and then shut it. Fritz was behind the desk, looking at some paperwork. Reg walked over to the desk while tugging at the buttons on his shirt.

"I won't do this," he announced through bared teeth while he ripped the taped microphone off before slamming it onto the desk. "I won't be a part of this. Zachary's here at work, and he's on time. That's all that matters. Fire me if

33

you want, but I won't compromise my work ethic no matter what the reason is."

Fritz waved his hands in front of him. "Calm down. No one's asking you to compromise anything. You've clearly misunderstood. Let's just forget about it. How about we do lunch again today? Anywhere you want. You name it."

Reg was refastening the buttons on his shirt. "Don't know if you'll want to after you listen to the conversation Zachary and I just had." He nodded toward the recorder on Fritz's desk. "He and I will be going to lunch today."

Fritz pressed a button on the recorder. A second later, a tinny voice said, "Message has been deleted."

Fritz looked up at Reg. "What conversation would that be?"

Reg nodded. "If it's all the same to you, I'll keep my appointment with Zachary. Perhaps some other time."

"Of course," Fritz replied, eyes narrowed. "Maybe tomorrow."

* * *

Reg pulled the door shut behind him. Fritz waited a moment, then reached out and yanked up the receiver of the phone sitting on the desk. Keeping his voice low, he growled his irritation. "I have something I need for you to do. I'll meet you in ten minutes. You know where I'll be."

Chapter 7

Reg walked into Zachary's office at eleven forty-five. Brought a finger to his lips while handing Zachary a note. Zachary read it and he took it back. Crammed it in a pocket. "So are you ready to go?" he asked, kept his tone casual. Zachary nodded in spite of the okay-but-I-don't-get-it look. "Sure."

Reg could tell that he'd gotten the message—not to say a word about whatever it was he'd wanted to share with Reg earlier. Not until Reg said he could. On the way to Reg's car they talked about anything else. Even as they drove east through downtown Newark, away from Anderson Electric.

They kept the conversation casual as they drove down Broad Street and past a host of restaurants they'd visited before. At the corner of Broad and Market, Reg saw a place to park and pulled in.

Zachary got out. Reg did too, but not before he reached into the backseat to get his briefcase. With an I-don't-believe-you look, Zachary said, "Do you ever go anywhere without that?"

"How long have you known me?" came Reg's lighthearted reply.

"Right."

They walked along until they came to the lower plaza of a taller office building. "Ah," Zachary acknowledged when Reg made the turn to go up the steps. "Luigi's. We haven't come here in a while."

"We haven't done lunch in a while." A lot had changed after Anna's diagnosis.

Reg flashed a few bills, and they were led straightaway to a back booth. He slid in one side, set his briefcase underneath; Zachary settled in across from him.

"Okay," Reg said. "You can talk now."

Zachary looked around instead. "First off, what's with all the secrecy and paranoia?"

"Precautions."

The waiter came back with two glasses of water and a polite request for their orders. They both ordered the lunch special: three-cheese pasta primavera with a garden salad. With the waiter gone, Zachary spoke again. "Trying to keep Fritz happy I guess?"

Reg sipped his water. "Just don't want to give him any more to think about. It'll probably be a while before he's convinced you're back on track. You are back on track, right?"

Zachary stared into his water while he swirled the lemon slice in it around with a straw. "Sure."

"Well, what were you so excited about this morning? Haven't seen that kind of enthusiasm from you in a while. Did you hear some good news about Anna's cancer?"

A slow smile formed on Zachary's lips. "You could say that. More than good news, actually...."

Zachary's longer-than-expected pause made Reg ask, "You going to make me wait forever? Lunch is only an hour you know."

"I guess I just don't know how to start."

"We're old friends. It shouldn't be that hard."

The waiter came back with their salads. Zachary waited until he left. "Okay, but you're not going to believe it."

Contemplative, Reg chewed a forkful of spinach, "Try me," he said after he swallowed.

"Well, first of all, Anna's gone." Zachary said this with the same heavy-hearted tone someone might when speaking of someone dear who'd passed.

"Again?"

"No. Not again. Forever. The Anna you saw last night wasn't Anna at all. It was an entity of some sort that has taken over her body and is going to give birth to our son … my son—"

Reg swallowed his second bite. Sipped his water. "You're right. I don't believe you. Try again."

"It's true, Reg. Every bit of it. Anna's gone and this entity is going to facilitate the birth."

Reg grabbed his napkin, wiped his mouth, then threw the napkin onto the tabletop. "Where do you get off telling me a story like that? It's one thing to believe something because you don't want to face the truth. It's another to believe something so absurd—so absolutely insane—and then to talk about it like it really happened. I'm worried about you, Zachary. This is too much."

"I can prove it. Anna's gone and something else—no, *someone* else—has taken over her body."

Reg glanced around. His forehead wrinkled to the point of pain in a frown, he turned back. "Look. I know you're under a lot of stress, but don't crack on me now. You'll make it through this. You will."

"Anna's gone, Reg. And this—entity, this other being, took over her form. She and Anna made a deal."

"She? This other being is a she?"

37

"Yes."

Reg let the answer hang, picked up his fork, then sighed. "Okay, I'll humor you. But keep in mind you're walking a very thin line. Just what sort of *deal* did the two make?"

"The entity would inhabit Anna's form, thus allowing for the birth of our son—and hers."

Reg, still holding his fork, now dropped it as though it were molten hot lava. Shoved a hand into an inside jacket pocket and came out with his cell phone. Zachary immediately wrapped fingers around the wrist that held the phone. "What're you going to do, Reg? Give Fritz a reason to fire me?"

Reg's finger hovered over the keypad.

"He will, you know. And I need this job. You're right. I didn't think about that last night. But my mind is clear now."

"That's debatable."

"Look, Reg. I wouldn't risk losing everything by telling you something as bizarre as this. Not unless it were true. If I were crazy, yes. But, Reg, I'm not crazy. And I can prove this. That's why I was so excited about telling you this morning."

Reg eased his finger away from the keypad. Zachary turned loose of his wrist. Reg put the phone away.

"You come to my house after work, and I'll do just that. I'll prove it to you, Reg."

"Fine. Until then, I'd prefer not to hear any more about it."

Zachary agreed, and the two finished their lunches in relative silence.

* * *

Back at the office, each went about their work. A little after five, Zachary left. Reg didn't leave until a little later. Reg pulled up at Zachary's close to seven-thirty.

Zachary responded to the knock and Reg followed him in. "Anna," Zachary called out.

"I thought you said at lunch that Anna was gone."

Zachary turned to face him. "Anna made me promise I'd help the entity. That means treating her as though she were Anna so no one gets suspicious."

Anna walked in from the kitchen. Stopped moving when she saw Reg. Disbelief swept over her face like a dark cloud.

"I can explain," Zachary said as though he could stop the brewing storm with his words.

"This is not good," she said, glared at Reg. "This is very bad." The cloud grew darker.

"I know you said not to tell anyone, but I had to. I have to know I'm not crazy. Can you not see that?"

She shook her head back and forth. Stared at Reg and Zachary in turn.

"How can one other person knowing the truth really be that bad?" Zachary continued. "I trust this guy. I'd trust him with my life—"

Placing a hand on Zachary's arm, Reg said to her, accusing, "What have you been telling him, and how did you manage to convince him a single word you've said is true?"

Her arm came up level with her shoulder. Her hand extended out toward him. Reg, who'd never been struck by lightning, felt as though that was what just happened. Zachary, too late with his warning, watched in horror while Reg took the jolt standing up, then collapsed on the ground when Anna lowered her arm and yelled, "Very, *very* bad!"

Chapter 8

Reg massaged the crick in his neck and sat up. Why was he on Zachary's couch in Zachary's living room? And why did his entire body tingle as though a thousand tiny pins were poking at him?

Zachary spoke from the bottom of the stairs. "How're you feeling?"

He turned, then grimaced. "How am I feeling? How am I supposed to be feeling? What happened?"

"Anna happened."

He squinted as he began to recall. "Oh yeah. Where is she now?"

"Charging."

"Charging?"

"Yeah, come on." Zachary motioned with a hand. "I'll show you."

Unsteady, Reg stood. "Wait a minute. Last time I followed you, I ended up on your floor and then your couch—with a sore neck. What makes you think I want to follow you again?"

Zachary seemed to consider that. He then walked over to where Reg had been standing *before* Anna zapped him. He bent down and then straightened. "Because I have your briefcase."

Not waiting for Reg's reply, he turned and headed back toward the stairs. "You'll have to come get it if you want it back."

It wasn't Zachary's I-have-something-you-want antic that had Reg moving. His curiosity did the job. And as far as being worried about his safety, Reg believed Zachary wouldn't lead him into harm's way intentionally.

At the top of the staircase, Zachary disappeared through a doorway. Reg stopped just short of going in. From where he stood he could see Anna on the bed. In that position he could clearly make out the defined upward bulge of her lower abdomen due to her pregnant state. More dramatic he guessed because she carried twins.

The sight would have seemed normal, except each of her hands was duct taped around two separate clamps that extended from ...

A battery charger plugged into the wall?

From what he could tell, Zachary had put medical gauze between the skin of her hands and the adhesive of the tape.

"It's how she charges," Zachary explained from where he stood at the foot of the bed. "Electrical energy's what sustains her. But we have to find another way."

Mesmerized, Reg moved farther into the room. Stopped next to Zachary, who'd walked around to the head of the bed. "See here on her neck? That's from last night."

Flummoxed, Reg noticed that the blistered burn marks were still an angry red.

"Last night she gave me instructions on how to contrive a charger of sorts with two butter knives and a utility cord."

He pointed, and Reg saw the contraption lay in a heap nearby.

"We came up with the battery-charger idea together. There's got to be a better way to keep this from happening, and this is a beta test."

Zachary spoke casually, as though there was nothing odd about it at all. Just another electrical problem to solve for one of the brightest electrical engineers in the country. Reg fixed him with a hard stare. Wanted to make sure he understood. "You do realize I'm not onboard with any of this? I just followed you up here because I was curious. I don't even know what's going on!"

"Well that's what I'm trying to explain. This is how she charges—"

"I know what you said," Reg snapped. "You don't have to repeat it. And even if you did repeat it, it doesn't make me want to believe it more. As far as I'm concerned, everything you've told me so far is *still* crazy talk. All of it. Every bit of it."

Looking toward Anna's form, Zachary said, "I'm not crazy. This is real. No human could withstand the voltage being delivered to Anna's body presently. But it's what keeps the entity alive."

Reg gave a sigh that, to his ears, sounded like a groan. "Suppose it is true. Which I'm not saying. But if it were exactly as you've explained, then how, Zachary, *how* can you just let *your* Anna go like that? If she's not in there," he motioned to the form on the bed, "and she's truly gone ... how can you do that?"

Then, trying to sound as sympathetic as he could, "How do you know that, that *thing,* or entity, or whatever it is, didn't kill her?"

"It didn't kill her, Reg. If anything, it gave her a few more weeks here with me."

Reg stared, mystified, as he continued. "Remember when they put Anna in the hospital so she could pass in comfort? Because the cancer was spreading that fast?"

Reg did in fact recall that. He'd gone to sit with Zachary when he could get a spare moment from work.

"Remember the night she had that miraculous turnaround that no one could explain, not even her doctors? Well, that's when it came to Anna. Anna said—"

"Anna said? You said she was gone—"

"Yes. A memory of her yesterday," Zachary said carefully. "It said that very near the end, Anna prayed. Prayed that her children be spared. She prayed and it—or rather *she* was sent. Electric Angel, that's what Anna called her."

Reg took a long moment to think about this. "And Anna told you during this—this memory of her."

Zachary swiveled his head, peered at Anna's hands, then turned back to Reg. "Yes. After you left yesterday. After she returned from being gone that day. I didn't want to believe any of it either. Who would? But then I was allowed access to Anna's memories just before she passed. I don't how it happened. I just know that Anna explained it all. Everything. And her final request was that I please help in raising the boys."

Reg couldn't shield his skepticism in time, and Zachary responded, his voice passionate, "She stayed at a motel. There was a storm, and the entity was thrown off track and destroyed the neon sign in front of it. Blew it right up. I called the motel and verified everything that happened. Everything, Reg. It's all real. It's all true."

Reg glanced at him, then back at the form on the bed. "An angel, you say?"

"That's how Anna referred to her."

"Some angel. It nearly killed me downstairs."

"She saw you as a threat."

"I see *her* as a threat."

A slow smile found its way to Zachary's lips. "You said *her*. You believe me."

A slow intake of breath, an even slower exhale. "Maybe."

Zachary walked across the room. "Let me show you something." He flipped off the light switch, then closed the bedroom door. Night had fallen. The room was aptly dark: except for Anna's abdomen. Which glowed.

Suddenly fighting for his next breath, Reg managed, "What ... what is that?"

"Anna and I learned early on that one of the twins would be stillborn if not absorbed by the body."

Reg nodded. "Yes, I remember you telling me that."

"The entity was with child as well—or with angel, depending on how you want to look at it. Anyway, her offspring now exists in that form. The way I understand it, he's responsible for the glow. That's him. Let me see if I can get a bigger reaction."

Zachary put a hand back on Anna's abdomen. The glow intensified, and then brightly flashed. He grinned. "One of them kicked."

Reg couldn't remove his eyes from the sight. "What about the other, ah ... the other fetus? How is it—him ... how is he surviving with all this electrical current?"

"She protects him. She keeps the level steady and tolerable for him. Here," Zachary nodded toward the entity's glowing belly. "Put your hand here, and I'll see if I can get one of them to kick for you."

Reg stared hard at the battery charger. "I don't think so. If she's got current running through her ..."

"I put a rubber mat down." Zachary pointed at what he was standing on. "Just step here."

His movements tentative, Reg did as Zachary said, then placed his hand alongside Zachary's. A tiny but very recognizable thump greeted him.

"Whoa, I felt that," he said. "That's ... amazing."

Zachary moved his hand around. Prodded gently. "Let me see if I can get the other one to kick. I have to warn you though, if I can get him to react, you'll feel a little sting—a bit of a shock. The mat doesn't help as much with him."

"Him? So he's like her," Reg whispered.

"Oh yes, in every way. Well, in every nonphysical way."

The glowing intensified, then flashed. Reg yanked his hand away and rubbed at his wrist. But he couldn't deny what he'd felt. "You're right."

"So you believe me. And you'll help me."

"I don't know how I can possibly help. But yes, I can see that something very out of the ordinary's going on here."

Anna's eyes fluttered open. "I can charge on my own now," she said to Zachary, then caught sight of Reg at the end of the bed. "He's here again."

"Yes," Zachary said. Turned the charger off. Pulled gently at the tape that secured her hands to the clamps.

"Why?"

"I want to talk to you again about letting him help."

Reg braced for a jolt like he received downstairs. Stood solid on the rubber mat just in case.

"You need someone to confide in," Anna said as though she didn't truly understand but might accept the fact if he convinced her.

"Yes, that's exactly what I need." She didn't nod, but tilted her chin; that encouraged him. "It would be so much easier for me to help you if Reg were allowed to stay."

She nodded then. Reg noticed, yet her expression remained hard to read. Finally she said, "If it helps you, then he can stay."

Zachary's smile revealed his relief. Reg chose to remain cautious. He stood to suffer more than Zachary if Anna changed her mind.

Chapter 9

At ten thirty-five, twenty minutes after leaving Zachary's house, Reg's headlights played across the stone marker of his subdivision. Three speed humps later and a turn to the right, he'd reached his townhome at the end of a cul-de-sac. He navigated the short driveway and parked in the garage. Carrying his briefcase and a bag that now only contained trash from the quick meal he'd consumed on the way home, he entered the kitchen via his laundry room. He tossed the bag into a trashcan just outside the back door and went inside. A lamp on a timer set to come on at 6 P.M. amply lit the way.

He walked to his study and set his briefcase down, slipped behind a desk that dominated the room, sat and swiveled around to face his computer. With a click of the mouse the screen popped on.

After what he'd experienced tonight, there was no doubt something had taken over Anna's body.

But what?

And where in the world should he start his search? He'd gone to seminary for two years because at one time he thought he wanted to be a minister. He decided later that this background must have influenced his decision to search for information about angels, and more specifically, the instance in Genesis 6 where angelic beings took human

47

form. Zachary said Anna referred to this entity as her electric angel, and while there was no reason to suspect she meant this literally, it at least gave him a place to start searching for sanity in the midst of such madness.

* * *

At work the next day a yawn forced his jaw open. Afterward, Reg took a long sip of lukewarm coffee, his second cup so far that morning. At some point during the night, he'd fallen asleep at his computer. Somewhere around four he woke up and realized he could no longer pull all-nighters as he used to do in college.

Hell, admit it, you could barely do it in college. He turned in his chair, opened a bottom filing cabinet drawer and reached for a file. His senses dulled from a lack of sleep, he didn't hear when someone came to stand in his doorway. He jumped when Fritz said, "I called your cell several times last night but didn't get an answer."

Reg was using a spare cell. His other cell shorted out when Anna zapped him. "Yeah. I dropped it," he lied. Probably not very convincing, but it wasn't in him to try harder. "I'm using this older phone until I can get a new one. I had to charge it, probably forgot to turn it back on."

Fritz nodded. "No biggie, we can talk now. Saw that our man Zachary was here again this morning. Bright and early. Good job."

His boss' words were positive. So why did he feel that Fritz was going somewhere negative with this? "He's back on track. No need to worry."

"I'd say I was more curious than anything. How did you do it?"

"Zachary's a reasonable man. I told you that."

Fritz took a step into the office and a seat across from Reg. "I'm still curious. What in the world did you do to convince him he should shirk his wife's illness, *and* show up at work on time? And in high spirits more or less. Or at least not as downcast as he's been the past few months. Do share."

Reg looked down at his desktop, shifted a few papers around. "I'm really busy. I don't have time for chitchat. Not if you want me to do my job, that is."

Fritz glared in reply. Reg didn't think this would be the end of it.

Then, the tension in Fritz' face eased up. "Fair enough," he said, moved to the edge of his seat. "But I want to hear more later."

* * *

Work dragged on. Reg stayed busy and at the same time managed to stay away from Fritz. Or perhaps Fritz had forgotten about talking to him. Either way, he was glad. He hated to lie but of course there was no other way. He couldn't tell Fritz the truth. First the men with butterfly nets would come, then the straitjackets. Then, quite possibly, the unemployment line.

When five o'clock rolled around, he moved to pack his briefcase and just when he thought he'd gotten away without having to talk to Fritz, the man appeared at his door. "You weren't about to leave were you?"

"Actually I was. Why?"

Fritz shrugged. "Nothing really. I just had something I wanted you to look into. Some background work I wanted you to do on a potential employee."

"It can't wait?"

"I suppose it could. It's just that you usually hang around longer than I do. Guess I'm spoiled. I'll just get with you in the morning." He took a step away, but then stopped. "Enjoy your evening."

49

As Reg walked to his car he couldn't ignore the feeling Fritz knew something. But how could he? He'd handed the wire back, and he'd been extra careful with his words all day today. Certain he was worrying about nothing, he got into his car and made his way out of the parking garage. After two blocks, he noticed a dark blue sedan behind him. It followed him for the next three blocks, and even when he randomly turned down a side street, always staying about two car lengths behind. When Reg sped up, the sedan did.

He looked ahead. A stoplight in front of him had just changed from green to caution. He slowed down as though he were going to stop, then sped up just as the caution light flashed to red. The sedan had to stop because the car in front of it did. Reg easily slid down two side streets and into another parking garage before the light changed again. He didn't leave until he was convinced he lost whoever followed him.

Zachary was waiting on his porch when Reg pulled up. He looked at his watch. "What took you so long? I thought you'd be here by now. Did you get caught up at work?"

"Yeah," Reg said walking to meet him. "Fritz had something he wanted me to do." When Zachary turned to open the door, Reg looked back at the street, saw no cars, dark or otherwise, and followed him inside.

Zachary shut the door and moved ahead of Reg toward the stairs. "Well I'm glad you're here now. I've got an idea on how to make the charging process simpler for Anna. Come on, I'll show you—"

Reg grabbed Zachary by a shoulder and pulled him around so Zachary faced him. "I think Fritz knows something. I'm not sure what, but something. I think he tried to keep me at work on purpose. And I'm pretty sure I was followed when I left. I ditched whoever it was, I think, but I have to tell you, it's got me a little on edge."

Zachary took a second to absorb this. "I don't get it. I've been showing up at work."

"I know, but I think Fritz might be thrown off by your recent change in attitude. For the past few months you've been about as down as a person can be—and rightly so. Yet overnight it seems you've had this huge turn with no explanation. And honestly, I can see where he might be curious."

Zachary's head fell forward.

"I'm not trying to make you feel bad, Zachary. There's no hiding how deeply you cared for Anna—"

Before he could finish, Zachary turned his back to him. His shoulders sank, as though an enormous wave had crashed down on him.

"I—I'm sorry," Reg said at Zachary's shoulders heaving beneath deep sobs, wondering how Zachary had been holding this inside.

"You have no right to judge me," Zachary finally said. "And Fritz doesn't either. Anna was everything to me."

Reg felt horrible. "I didn't mean to infer otherwise. It wasn't my intention at all. We just need to come up with a way to help others understand the change in you *without* letting the truth out."

Zachary nodded. Took a deep breath. "Yes. Maybe if we put our heads together we can come up with something."

When Zachary turned around to face him, Reg moved on. "When I got here you said you had something to show me?"

"Yes. In the basement."

Zachary led and Reg followed.

* * *

Anna stood close to the bottom of the basement stairs.

51

Zachary walked past her.

Reg didn't.

"You've come to help Zachary," Anna said casually. "I know he appreciates your company."

Still Reg stood on the step where he'd stopped.

Zachary glanced over his shoulder. "Well come on. She won't hurt you."

"And I'm sorry about last night," she added.

Trying to take that as consolation, Reg continued on down but cautiously side-stepped around her.

"Here's what I've come up with," Zachary said once Reg reached his side. He stood in front of a wet bar. The few things on the bar had been pushed to the side to make room. A soldering iron sat heating. A roll of solder rested near it. What looked like a power supply lay disassembled, or rather, reassembled. Reg decided it was the latter.

Zachary reached for and held up the results of his soldering, a two-inch round metal disk attached by solder onto a long electrical cord extending out of the power supply. "This end is a magnet."

Next, he picked up a metal disk about two inches wider than the magnet he held. "The idea is to insert this piece of metal under Anna's skin, but leave enough of it exposed so this magnet can be attached."

It seemed to Reg that Zachary had thought this all out, almost. But the way he mentioned inserting the metal disk under Anna's skin … as though it were just that simple. Reg said, "You don't just slide a piece of metal under the skin and call it a day. You sort of have to know what you're doing."

Zachary's enthusiasm visibly faded. "I … suppose I hoped you could help me find a way."

Reg relaxed his stance. "I'm sure we can find a way. It

does seem like what you've put together here will make the charging process easier."

The phone rang. Zachary looked at the caller ID. "It's Anna's oncologist." When he didn't answer, the machine began recording.

When the doctor had finished speaking and a click indicated he hung up, Reg looked at Zachary in shock. "You've not talked to him? According to that message she's missed two appointments."

Zachary shrugged. "I didn't know what to tell him."

How could Reg argue with that? He wouldn't know what to say himself. But the fact that the doctor called after office hours worried him. "Seems clear we need to tell him something." He turned to face Anna but spoke to Zachary. "You need to make an appointment. He needs to see Anna for himself."

"Too risky. Fully charged, she might electrocute someone if they just touch her. And what will we do about her abdomen? We're used to it, but anyone who isn't is going to wonder about the glow."

"I can do it," Anna blurted, walked over to where the two men stood. "It isn't like I didn't know the difficulties I'd have when I chose to consider Anna's help. I knew there would be issues with how much energy I could store at once. I also knew I wouldn't be able to regenerate my own electrical energy, as I can when I'm not in this form. I've much more control now. Here, I'll show you."

She extended a hand out for Reg to take. Reg gulped, then hesitantly took her hand. A broad smile spread across his face. "I didn't feel anything. Not even a light shock."

"And that's with a full charge," she added.

"Call the doc back, make the appointment," he said to Zachary. "Let me know when it is so I can make sure Fritz

53

understands you haven't fallen into your old ways."

He reached down, picked up his briefcase and headed toward the stairs. "Don't know about you, but I've had maybe three hours' sleep in the last twenty-four. Call me later. Leave a message if you have to but make sure and let me know about the appointment."

Chapter 10

At 9:20 P.M. Fritz sat at his desk, pressed the appropriate buttons on his cell and listened to the recording again. He'd listened to it five times already and still found it difficult to believe. Deciding he'd heard it enough times, he pulled up the desk phone and called up another number.

"Wonderful work," he said to the one who answered. "Now I've got something else for you to do. But I don't want to tell you over the phone. Let's meet at the usual spot. This task won't be so easy, but I can assure you if you make it worth my while, it will certainly be worth yours."

* * *

The meeting Fritz called the next morning surprised even Reg. Fritz wanted to discuss the bid Anderson Electric had won to supply cheap energy to the inner-city housing projects. When Anderson Electric scored the bid, all Fritz could do was complain. The company didn't stand to make any money off this project. The only guarantee was that what little money came in would be consistent.

So why did Fritz seem so happy this morning? Why was he suddenly the cheerleader for a project he absolutely hated? The only meetings he'd had so far concerning it involved ways to cut corners. Reg couldn't wait for the meeting to end so he could question Fritz about his change of heart. He thought he'd wait until the room cleared, as he usually did when he wanted to speak privately to him, but Fritz had other plans.

"Reg," he said coming to stand next to him while everyone listened. "I want you to be my lead man on this project."

"Shouldn't that position be given to one of the engineers?" That's the way things usually happened.

"No," Fritz said. "You're the man for this job. No doubt about it. And as that man, I want you to meet me in my office in an hour."

* * *

Anna's appointment with her oncologist happened the very afternoon after Zachary called. The oncologist immediately scheduled tests to be run. For the two days it took to get the results back, Anna was told to stay on her medication, or rather, to get back on it, until they had the results. An order she ignored.

Two days later, Zachary, Anna and Reg went to hear the results. With a look that screamed *I-don't-believe-it*, the doctor glanced once more at the test results clipped inside a medical folder before closing it and removing his reading glasses to settle himself onto the edge of his desk. Zachary and Anna looked on from the two chairs next to each other; Zachary clasped her left hand with his right one. He fidgeted his fingers in an anticipatory manner, even though he already knew what the tests would say.

"Don't keep us in suspense."

"Yes," Reg added, sounding anxious as well. "What did you find out?"

"I'm sorry. I guess I'm still trying to take it all in. It's just so, well—amazing. I've looked over these test results again and again, certain there had to be some mistake. Checked with the radiologist and lab director too. But there's no mistake." An unbidden laugh punctuated this observation. "Anna's cancer, or rather what little is left of it, appears to be in remission. It's as if whatever happened to her in the hospital a few days ago happened again, but on a much grander scale. It's nothing short of miraculous."

Though the entity, by its own admission, could eradicate all the cancer from Anna's body, both Zachary and Reg felt it would be smarter not to do so until after the doctor visit. Otherwise the miracle would be so grand, it might bring her under even more scrutiny and more tests. Something they didn't want. It had to remain a common miracle, one that had happened before but not too extreme.

Zachary played his part well and beamed appropriately upon hearing the test results. "Your prayers worked, Anna."

The doctor added, "Indeed. I certainly can't think of anything else to cause such a turnaround."

Anna smiled as well. Placed a maternal hand on her pregnant abdomen. "I just wanted my children to have a chance. The prayers weren't for my sake," and then to the doctor, "when will I need to see you again?"

"I'd like to see you in a month. In the meantime, take half the dosage of the medicines I had you on, and start regular visits to your obstetrician if you haven't arranged for that already." His eyes shifted to her bulging abdomen. "From the last time I've seen you, I'd say your pregnancy is progressing as quickly as your cancer is receding."

* * *

They held it together even as they exited, and didn't drop the façade until they were at street level. "I'd say that went well," Zachary said, held the car door open for Anna.

"Yeah," Reg replied, his voice not as emotion packed as his friends'.

57

"Something wrong?" Zachary asked while he closed the car door behind Anna.

A tight-lipped smile found its way to Reg's face. "No. Why?"

"I just expected you to be happier I guess."

He shrugged. "I'm happy," he said, hesitated, then tossed his briefcase into the front seat. "Now let's get back to the office before Fritz gets suspicious and talks about letting you go again."

Zachary slid in next to Anna and pulled the door closed behind him. Reg walked around the back of the car and spoke under his breath without fear of being heard. "If you knew what I knew you wouldn't be happy either."

Chapter 11

Roughly six weeks later, Reg sat at his desk attempting to stay calm. He'd been woken up at four that morning when Zachary called to tell him that Anna's water had broken.

A month after Anna's seeming miracle, the oncologist took her off all her medication, since the tests now revealed she was cancer free. He didn't order further tests and released her from his care, saying her obstetrician could follow her from this point. Which wouldn't happen, but the oncologist having served his usefulness and remaining in blissful ignorance, all three simply nodded at his instruction.

With this dilemma out of the way, Zachary and Reg could concentrate on other matters. How to deliver a baby, or rather two? They both acknowledged there would be serious problems having the delivery at a hospital. And hiring a midwife would be far too risky as well, if they didn't want to let anyone else in on their secret.

Anna, having no memory of a previous childbirth, only cared about keeping the secrecy of the event, and her. She listened with mild interest while the men discussed how best to prepare themselves for the intimidating task of assisting with the delivery, with both acknowledging, when it seemed an overwhelming venture, that childbirth was after all a natural event and women had done it for centuries without any help at all. Armed with that, and with Anna now eight months pregnant, they could only complain about the amount of time they had left to learn.

And now, Reg realized there was no time left.

"I don't see any reason for you to rush over, though," Zachary added. "I'll call you when it looks like things are moving along."

Lunch went by without a call. Somewhere around four, the phone rang. In spite of expecting it and having constantly glanced at it all day, Reg jumped in his seat.

"She's having contractions," Zachary told him.

Reg said he'd be right over, returned the phone to its cradle, leaned down to pick up his briefcase—but stopped before he did and stared at it, as though it made a difference whether he took it along or not. Of course he rationalized that not taking it would matter now. The damage had already been done. Not taking it would only mean more problems.

Accepting the consequences his actions had brought, Reg reached down, picked it up, and begrudgingly took his briefcase, his constant companion turned albatross, along with him.

* * *

Reg set his briefcase down and headed over to where Anna lay on her side. "How far apart are they?" he'd asked upon entering the dark bedroom. Zachary had done everything to provide a calming environment for Anna, as everything they read insisted they should. The windows had thick curtains to block any light from getting in, and thank God, from getting out. If not, anyone walking behind the house might wonder about the intermittent flashes of light.

Her abdomen glowed intensely now, and flashed brilliantly every few seconds. Anna lay silent and focused on the task.

"That's really something," Reg said, watching the light show.

"I know," Zachary said. "It started shortly after her water broke, and it hasn't let up."

Reg looked around the room. "With it as dark as it is in here, it resembles a lightning storm. Like lightning in a bottle, but really it's lightning in a belly." He tried to laugh at his joke but reality kept that response in check. The situation was simply too serious. Instead he walked to the end of the bed, hands previously scrubbed, and pulled a latex glove from a box to check Anna's progress. He recalled what a friend who worked as a midwife told him about how to properly check for dilation. A finger represented one centimeter. Somewhere around ten centimeters the urge to push would be great.

Reg straightened. "Not there yet, but I don't think it'll be much longer."

Anna remained silent, eyes closed, concentrating on her important task: bringing two healthy babies into the world. Reg settled into one of two wingback chairs arranged on either side of a small round table adjacent to the bed. "Guess all we can do is wait now and hope for the best."

Zachary sank into the other chair and nodded.

Neither man felt fear, except the fear that they wouldn't perform well at the procedure they had rehearsed at least a dozen times, and discussed countless times. Both knew that when Anna was actually giving birth, there was a chance, if slight, that she might lose control of her senses—and of the powerful electrical charge within her body. But each of them accepted that, barring the additional rubber mats on the floor and as much caution as they could use, there was nothing they could do but hope neither of them were electrocuted.

An hour went by. Anna turned onto her back from her side. When she cried out, both men leaped up. Zachary headed over to the end of the bed. Made quick work of donning a set of latex gloves. He glanced beneath the sheet draped over Anna's legs.

"Something's happening," he said. "I—I can see a head."

Standing on one of the rubber mats spread around the room, Zachary reached under the sheet. Reg, hands gloved as well, stood close by. In his trembling fingers he held a pair of sterilized scissors. He used them to cut the cord when Zachary pulled the first infant from under the sheet. The riskiest part of the entire operation was halfway over.

Without any prodding, the infant gasped for his first breath. Zachary beamed pride. "Look Reg. It's my son."

But in that short moment, the room had grown dark. Anna's abdomen no longer glowed. Zachary looked down at the child he held. It no longer breathed. Frantic, he turned toward Anna.

"W-what's wrong, Anna? Is something wrong?"

"They need each other," she told him, her voice weak.

"But I don't understand. What do I do?"

She was either too weak to respond or didn't know. In her stead, Reg took the child Zachary held and carefully placed him on Anna's abdomen. The glowing recommenced. The infant kicked and began breathing once more. And Anna's abdomen heaved.

Zachary reached under the sheet to deliver the second twin. After cutting the cord, he placed the infant beside his brother once he heard it take its first breath. "Fancy that, they look exactly alike," he said in wonder.

"Minus the hair," Reg observed. The second twin had none. Not even eyebrows. "Are they both normal?" The differences were enough to make him wonder.

Puzzled, Zachary asked, "What do you mean?"

"Well, they'll need to eat soon. We didn't really consider if there'd be anything different we need to do for them, or even just the one."

"Yes, I suppose we hadn't given that any thought."

Anna, head slightly lifted to admire the infants cradled on her belly, said, "They will both eat normally, but the one that is like me will need to maintain a certain level of electrical current. Together they can create enough electrical current though."

"How?" Zachary asked.

As if to answer, the first-born reached out to the other. A spark shot out at the initial touch, and the second twin's eyes began to glow.

Reg's look turned anxious at the sound of car doors opening and closing outside. "Is there anything else, Anna? Anything else we should know—about the boys?"

"No," she said, squinting at Reg.

The closed door to the bedroom flew open. "Nobody move!"

Five gun-wielding men dressed in black, faces covered, rushed in.

"Get away from the bed!" one of them screamed at Zachary, waving his gun.

"No!" Anna cried out, physically unable to stop anything from happening. Not even when one man reached out for the infants.

Zachary only had time to jerk his head around before two of the men grabbed and restrained him.

"They need to be kept together," Reg yelled out over the infants, who had cried out the second they were taken up. "Just make sure to keep them physically close to each other. But hurry! I don't know how long we have. The others'll be here soon if not already."

One of two rubber-gloved, insulated-suited men handed his infant to a similarly dressed individual. The infants calmed instantly.

Zachary pulled at the ropes his attackers were using to tie him to a chair. "What's going on, Reg?"

Reg turned to face him. "I'm sorry," he said, following after the man holding the infants, who was almost at the door. "I didn't have a choice. Not a good one anyway—"

He turned at a voice in the hall that said, "Come on." He gave Zachary one final look, then grabbed up his briefcase and darted out, saying, "This is what's best. I promise. I'll do my best to take good care of them."

* * *

Zachary listened to the footfalls, heard at least four car doors opening and closing. He called out to Anna, but she didn't answer, and he doubted she would be able to untie him. He twisted his wrist around until he'd rubbed the skin raw, then sat quiet, the sound of his own breathing the only sound he could hear—and then he heard something else. Car doors opened and shut again. Footfalls on the stairs once more.

Reg must've come back. But why? To do something even worse? He tried think of how he could free himself, Anna made a sound. He turned toward her. For the second time in the space of maybe ten minutes, the bedroom door Reg had shut flew open once again. It wasn't Reg however; but they too had guns. One carried a box, a rectangular one banded with yellow-and-black caution stripes. A symbol Zachary

64

had seen plenty of times before.

Over Zachary's shouts, then pleading, one intruder shoved furniture out of the way to find an outlet, plugged it in. A red light came on and it began to hum. He went straight over to Anna's form and connected a dangling cable directly to the circular disk at the base of Anna's neck—the disk that he and Reg implanted to make the charging process easier for Anna. His heart sank, realizing how easy his invention had made the man's task.

A switch flipped, and Anna's form lurched. The man then set the box-like machine down and began to take a pulse. Another man went over to Zachary while several others ran back out, as though looking for something they hadn't found. When they came back empty handed the apparent leader barked at Zachary.

"Where are they?"

"I don't know what you're talking about," Zachary replied, though he did.

Zachary's head snapped to the side from the slap.

"Leave him alone," the man with the box said as he unplugged what he'd brought in. "What we have here will do. Let the boss man deal with whoever double-crossed him."

Dazed from the blow, Zachary couldn't prevent his head from lolling to the side. From somewhere in the hall he heard a voice say, "Let's go before a neighbor gets suspicious and calls the cops."

The footfalls faded a second time. Car doors opened and shut, followed by the low hum of engines as they were driven off.

"Anna," Zachary whispered, as he'd done after the first group left. "Anna, can you hear me?"

She remained silent. Dead silent.

Chapter 12

The rain fell at a steady pace and streaked the car windows as watery rivulets ran down them, in a race to catch each other. The sun hid behind dark, heavy clouds. The day had started out gloomy and remained that way. At four-forty in the afternoon, there was little hope this would change.

The two tiny passengers rode in silence in the backseat, two brothers, both seven years old. One stared out the rain-streaked window. The other simply stared ahead. On the road for nearly an hour and a half, they'd been told they were almost at their destination.

A few more miles down one road and two turns later, the car moved onto a gravel drive, passed a sign that read "Sunny Brook Children's Home," and eased to a stop in front of a one-story brick building with two similar buildings on either side of it. The rain had stopped. The man driving checked his reflection in the rearview mirror, then turned to the boys.

"You both understand why we have to do this, right?" Then, to the boy by the window who had nodded, "You explained it to him?"

He nodded again.

"Okay then, let's go. Oh, and make sure to keep the collars of your shirts turned up a little because—well, you know why."

A woman in her early thirties, brown shoulder-length hair, turned from the conversation she was having with an older woman, saw them, and walked directly over.

"You must be Paul." As Paul shook her hand in introduction, he revealed nothing that might hint he wasn't using his real name. "I'm Mary Little. It's so nice to finally meet you." She acknowledged the boys. "You must be Jeri and Mik. Why, you two do look just alike."

"Jeri with an 'I' at the end," Mik said.

"It's short for Jeremiah." Paul explained further, knowing the spelling was odd enough to warrant an explanation.

"He's Jeri," Mik said as if to clear up any confusion. All while Jeri stood silent, the near-mirror image of his brother except for the lack of body hair including eyelashes and eyebrows. Alopecia universailis, Paul explained to Martha in the phone conversation that had led to this meeting.

"I'd like to hear that from Jeri," Mary said.

"He doesn't talk much," Mik explained. "He's still learning."

"Still learning?" Mary turned to look at Paul. "We're really not equipped to deal with that sort of issue here—"

"Oh it's not an issue," Paul said, his words rushed. "He's just a little shy, and Mik has always spoken for him. You know how twins are. Jeri's quite capable of speech I assure you. Right, Mik?"

Mik nodded unconvincingly when nudged by Paul, but didn't comment further.

"I think I'd like to hear Jeri speak for himself," Mary said.

"Sure." Paul turned to the other boy. "Say something." When that didn't work, he said, "Why don't you tell her how old you are?"

"I'm seven," Jeri said as rehearsed. The clicking sound at the end of his sentence hardly noticeable unless you were listening for it.

"Now can we get on with things," Paul said. "I think it would be best not to drag it out any longer—for the sake of the boys of course."

"Of course," Mary replied, then turned to the woman she'd been talking with before the three came in. "Patsy, can you show Jeri and Mik to the recreation room so we can get things in order here?"

The boys followed Patsy out the door and just around the corner. "Someone will come for you shortly," Patsy instructed, barely making an effort to sound as though she understood how they must feel. "Just stay here until they do." With no more talk, she left.

A chest of donated toys sat against a far wall, untouched, over which a white piece of poster board hung. Colorful markers had been used to spell out, "Please Keep Play Area Clean." A television mounted on a wall nearby babysat a small group of children ranging in ages from seven to ten. From where the two boys stood beside an air vent, if they listened close, they could still hear what was being said in the room they just left.

Paul's voice filtered through. "You don't seem to understand. They need to stay together. You told me this was possible when I called."

Mary spoke next. "What I told you was that we are a volunteer organization. We do our best with the money we have. I'm sure I told you that we'd do what we could to facilitate your request, but we couldn't promise anything. We don't have room to keep the boys together at this time. They'll be in the same building though, and have contact with each other. And when we have room, we'll put them together. They'll be fine."

"Do you think this is some sort of game? I want them together for a reason. I wouldn't have made such big deal about it otherwise."

"I wish I could accommodate you, but it just wouldn't be fair to the other children who've been here longer."

They heard Paul sigh and for a moment, nothing else. Then Paul spoke once more. "I guess I'll just bring them back when you can assure me you can keep them in the same room."

Mik whispered to Jeri, "What should we do? His plan isn't working. We won't be together."

Jeri held out a hand, looked toward a wall outlet very near where they stood. Mik nodded. "Yes, you're right. It's worth trying anyway."

* * *

Mary's voice squawked over the archaic intercom system, "Patsy could you come to the front—"

She stopped talking when the lights dimmed, then flashed to darkness. The sound of a transformer blowing rocked the building. Startled screams erupted from the rec room.

Mary reached under a cabinet and retrieved a flashlight. There were no windows in the hallways and a thick-clouded dusk settled outside. She flipped the flashlight on and headed toward the screams. Paul followed.

"Everybody calm down," she said upon entering. "Things will be back up and running shortly." Muted daylight filtered through blinds she quickly opened. "Go to the storeroom and get more flashlights," she directed an older boy, handing him hers. She then scanned the room for Mik and Jeri. "Has anyone seen the two boys Ms. Patsy

69

brought in here?"

Some shook their heads back and forth; others shrugged.

Patsy came to stand in the doorway. To Mary's question, she answered, "When I left the room they were standing right there."

With the room being as dark as it was, the charred electrical outlet didn't raise suspicions for anyone but Paul. "You lost them?" he said before anyone could notice him staring.

"They're here somewhere," Mary replied. "I'm sure of it. Where would they go?"

Yet after at least twenty minutes of searching closets and rooms, the boys were still missing.

A worried Mary asked, "Why would they leave?" She turned to Paul. "Do you have any ideas?"

He rubbed at the back of his neck, distracted. "No."

Lines creased her otherwise smooth forehead. "I don't know what else to do but to call the police. Of course we'll keep looking."

"I'll drive around the perimeter before it gets too dark," Paul offered. "Call me on my cell if you find them before I get back."

Chapter 13

The rain left deep puddles, and the boys found more than a few in their sprint to get away from Sunny Brook. They'd darted out a side door seconds after the transformer on a pole outside exploded.

Nobody noticed. Upon realizing this, they ran as far as they could into the woods across the street until they had to stop to catch their breath. Bent at the waist, hands on knees, Mik grinned over at Jeri. "That was—that was neat. I didn't know we could blow up something that big."

Jeri registered a weak grin, his eyes not as bright as they should be. "You need to charge." An anxious hand sank into a front pocket of Mik's jeans. "You need juice."

Mik held the end of a two-foot long cord. Let it uncoil. He reached around to attach the disk at one end to a similarly sized disk on the back of his neck. "Here," he said, and offered Jeri the other disk. Jeri didn't make a move to take it. "I know you don't like to do it this way, but it's quicker. And if we don't hurry—they might catch up. C'mon, you have to charge. You know what'll happen if you don't."

Mik settled his brother onto their two rain jackets he'd just spread out on the wet ground. "It'll be fine."

He attached the second disk to the back of Jeri's neck, then leaned against him for support.

71

Leaning against each other's backs, both boys began to glow.

* * *

Paul stood at the edge of the woods and stared. He suspected this was where the boys had fled. But after the stunt the boys pulled with the transformer, he knew Jeri would have to charge soon. Would he be able to see the glow from the charging process from where he stood? Doubtful. The boys were smarter than that, and careful as well. Other than that, any glow produced would be hard to see with it still being light out.

He stared a little longer out into the woods. But why had the boys run in the first place? He thought they understood.

After a few more minutes of considering, he headed back to his car. A woodsman, he wasn't. If he went into the woods now and tried to find them, he'd need a flashlight and a lot of luck. It made more sense to just drive around to the other side and wait for them to exit.

* * *

Still back to back, their hooded rain jackets spread out beneath them to protect from the damp earth, the glow that surrounded them as they charged dulled. Mik removed the magnetic disk, stood and offered his brother a hand getting up. Jeri's eyes shone brighter now.

"Better." Mik smiled as he pocketed the cable. "But we have to keep moving. It'll be real dark soon. We gotta find somewhere to hide. At least until morning anyway."

The woods grew thicker as they walked, then began to thin out. An embankment rose before them. They crept up it but stayed low to the ground as they crawled. Once at the top, Mik parted the taller grass. Across the way he identified a post office, a grocery store and donut shop. He turned to Jeri beside him and nodded. Both crawled back down.

"We need to get over there," Mik said. "Maybe if we go that way," he pointed where the woods thinned, "maybe there's a place to cross." He bit at his lip. "We have to hide you better, so people won't pay attention to you. You know, because you don't have hair." He puzzled for a moment. "I know. We can just pull your hood up."

When Jeri didn't do as Mik directed, Mik pulled his hood up for him. "Don't be scared. We'll be okay. Besides, she won't let nothing happen to us. Not to you anyway. And you won't let nothing happen to me." Jeri nodded as Mik tightened the cord to the hood so it wouldn't blow back in the breeze. "Now come on."

They trudged on, Jeri following after Mik until Mik yanked his brother by an arm behind a thicker patch of bushes. There was indeed a break in the woods beyond.

"See?" Mik said. "I was right. I bet that sidewalk goes to that road we saw. I'll bet there's lots of places to hide over there. C'mon."

Jeri pulled him back by an arm. "What?" Mik asked, his enthusiasm curbed. "Yeah, I guess you're right. We shouldn't cross alone. Maybe we could just follow somebody. You know, just stay behind them so they don't notice."

Foot traffic on the sidewalk didn't offer many possibilities, but eventually a prospect came along, a young man who looked in his twenties. He stopped directly in front of where the boys hunkered and lit a cigarette. Upon each exhale, the smoke drifted to where the boys hid. They both struggled not to cough. With ear buds firmly planted in both ears, the young renegade, pierced and tattooed, pulled a folded-in-half magazine from a back pocket and walked on. Mik pulled Jeri along, whispering, "Let's go."

They stayed far enough behind to keep from being noticed, crossed the main road when he did, and hung out behind the bus-stop pavilion until it seemed they could slip away unnoticed.

Mik considered the parking lot as they walked across. Off to their left he saw a battered pickup, the bed covered with a tarp, its hood up.

"C'mon," he said over his shoulder before he headed toward it. "We can hide in here." Under the tarp sat bag after bag stuffed full of aluminum cans, but room enough for the two of them if they scrunched in tight. "We can leave later when it's much darker. Until then we can rest."

They climbed in and pushed amongst the bags of cans for space. It wasn't long before they both fell asleep.

* * *

Paul, parked in a grocery store lot, scanned the line of trees near the edge of the road with binoculars. He'd been sitting there for about thirty minutes. Just like the last time he checked, he saw no movement that would indicate the boys were anywhere around.

He put the binoculars down to check his cell for missed messages. He called Sunny Brook when he saw he had none. At that same moment, a bus pulled up to the bus stop close to where he'd parked. As he spoke with Mary he watched a young man board, stopping just before getting on to crush out a cigarette beneath the toe of his shoe.

"So you've had no luck either," he said to Mary.

"No," she replied. "But the good news is the police promised they'd keep an eye out. I have a close friend on the force. He assured me they'd keep watching for them."

"I suppose I'll drive around some more as well. It's really getting too dark to see anything though. If they don't show up before morning, I'll start looking again." He ended the call, started his car and moved out onto the main road. He didn't check his rearview mirror as he moved along. Didn't see the two hooded figures hanging around just behind the bus-stop pavilion. When he finally did look, all he saw was the bus pulling away.

Where could they be? he thought as he headed back toward the motel he'd seen down the road.

* * *

Zachary walked with subdued trepidation down the long hall. Students from his last class filed past him. His Web assistant, Wesley, stopped him to get the key so he could lock up later that night.

"Yes, of course," Zachary obliged. This would free him up to do other things.

With nothing more on his mind, he rushed to his small office in the same building, quickly moved inside and locked the door behind him. Sitting in the chair behind his small desk, he pulled out the hand-addressed envelope that had him distracted all morning.

Earlier when he found it in his mail slot he envisioned himself tearing into it at once. Now, in the privacy of his office, all he could do was stare at it, asking the same question he'd asked all day: Who in the world could it be from?

He'd been living the life of a recluse since that tragic night when Anna died and the boys were kidnapped. He left his job at Anderson Electric shortly after, unable to function. In spite of the serious hit of the headhunter's fee, Fritz surprised him by giving him a hefty lump-sum severance package to help him along.

Months later, and deciding he couldn't depend on the lump sum forever, he considered a teaching job. A four-year college outside Newark contacted him after he applied for several positions, and eventually he signed on. He lived in an apartment just off campus grounds, and otherwise kept to himself. He'd grown accustomed to his mundane life. He only dreamed occasionally of the nightmare events that changed his life forever. Only speculated how things might be if things hadn't happened the way they did. Something about the mysterious letter made him think the contents might change that.

But then he laughed. *What are the odds of that after all these years?*

Envelope open and letter in hand, he read:

> *The boys are alive but in great danger. They are being taken to a safer place. You are to go pick them up after you receive another letter that will tell you where to find them. If all goes well you should receive that letter in a day or so.*

He gasped as though he'd been punched in the gut. Flipped the letter over to see if the signature missing from the letter might be there. It wasn't.

"Alive?" His brow furrowed. "How can that be?" *This has to be some kind of joke. Some kind of sick joke played by one of those fiends who kidnapped my son.* He directed his disgust at the one person he held responsible. How could Reg be so heartless?

Zachary wadded up the letter and launched it across the room. Then the envelope. The nightmare played out again as he sat at his desk in broad daylight, fighting tears he hadn't known he had left to shed.

The emotion, the pain, the anguish he'd kept pent up came spewing out like lava from a dormant volcano. "You son of a bitch," he screamed as he cleared the top of his desk with a broad, violent sweep of his arm. "How dare you?" Then again, as rage gave way to sobs. "How *dare* you?"

* * *

A squad car parked on either side of Carl Dotson's pickup, the one he had abandoned in the grocery store parking lot about a week ago. Unable to save up enough cash to buy the new battery it needed, it sat abandoned. Yet Carl always seemed to have cash to spend at the local liquor store. And even though he reeked of hard liquor presently, he insisted he was sober.

"I ain't been drinkin'. Everything's just like I tol' ya," Carl slurred as he pointed at what they'd found when they lifted a corner of the tarp. "I seen 'em climb in. I know'd they didn't think I seen 'em but I did."

Tom Sheppard, the officer who responded to the call with Deputy John Slayer, made a pathetic noise with his mouth and a pointed observation. "Yeah, well, last week you said you saw little green men pissin' in the bushes across the street from your trailer. And I won't even repeat what you said you saw the weekend before that."

"Yeah, well, I ain't seein' things tonight. I tol' you too. Besides, I ain't had a drink in," Carl held up a hand as if to count fingers but scowled instead. "I'm tellin' ya, I ain't drunk. You see the proof."

Deputy Slayer shined his light on the two hitchhikers in the bed of Carl's pickup. "But what the devil's wrong with that one?" Carl asked. "He ain't got no hair to speak of."

John Slayer ignored Carl and helped the two boys down

from the truck-bed. "Get Sunny Brook on the horn," he said to Tom. "Tell them we found their runaways. We'll have them back in a— son of a—" he cried out at the kick to his shin just before the two boys took off. "You come back here!"

When it was clear they weren't going to return at his request, John hobbled over to his squad car, jumped inside and slammed the door shut behind him.

The store had closed a half hour ago. John navigated the lot at top speed and easily made it to the end of the walkway that ran in front of the store before the boys could reach it. He turned the wheel hard and forced the car to fishtail, sufficiently blocking that exit. Tom pulled his car up to keep them from running back the other way. They were hemmed in as tight as fish in a rain barrel. The only escape now would be to run ahead and directly past the officers who'd left their cars to block that exit as well.

"You see here," John said, faced the two and tried not to scowl; his shin still ached from the kick. "We're only here to help you." He stopped at the edge of the large puddle that surrounded the two boys, water that had pooled from the rain earlier that day. The depth was such that it nearly covered their shoes. "You're too small to get away, so it doesn't make sense for you to run."

One step farther, and John and Tom were standing in the puddle as well, at the very edge.

The boys exchanged a quick sideways glance.

"That's right," John said. "The two of you think about it. There's no way out of this, so you might as well come along willingly."

John leaned to grab the one nearest him. Tom reached out for the other. The two boys rushed to join hands, and the puddle that all four now stood in instantly charged with

78

electricity. The two officers appeared as puppets on strings, then fell face first in the deep puddle, unconscious, when the boys released each other. Just as that happened, another squad car, already on its way, sped over and skidded to a stop. Seeing officers down, the two men inside jumped out and rushed forward.

Eyes wide, Carl hollered, "No! You step in that puddle you'll be electrocuted too. Just like they were."

Chapter 14

The coroner ruled both the officers' deaths as a drowning. But what had caused John Slayer and Tom Sheppard to fall unconscious into the deep puddle in the first place? A full day after the incident the only witness, Carl Dotson, still insisted the boys were responsible.

"That funny-lookin' boy," he said. "The one with no hair. He cut through the power cord of one'a them drink machines they was standing between. Then he laid the one end down into the puddle where Tom and John was standing."

Investigators went back and found the cut cord of the drink machine just as Carl had described, but they didn't find any knife, which surely the boys would have needed to cut a cord that thick and strong. The coroner confirmed that both Tom and John did receive a strong jolt of electricity, yet electrocution wasn't the cause of death. The new evidence was enough to warrant a hearing though, so the boys were assigned a state-appointed attorney. The hearing was scheduled for the following day and would continue until the judge decided he'd heard enough to make a ruling.

Because they were juveniles, details were hard to come by. A local paper posted updates without elaborating. Paul entered the convenience store a half block down from his motel. The paper would be delivered here first, at approximately 5:30 A.M.; Paul was told when he called to ask.

The storeowner nodded in his direction. "Paul," he acknowledged. "Got your coffee and your paper here."

Paul had grown comfortable with his alias, so didn't flinch or twitch, as he had at first. He put his money on the counter. "Keep the change."

"So what do you make of the hearing so far?" the storeowner asked. "Kind of funny to me, how quick things have been moving considering how slow things of this nature usually take."

Paul forced nonchalance. "The judge is probably trying to keep it low key since the boys are only seven. The hearing could turn into a media circus. I'm sure he doesn't want that."

Paul managed a few steps away from the counter before the storeowner spoke again. "Where do you suppose the parents are? Or even that guy who dropped them off at Sunny Brook and then disappeared?"

The comment gave Paul reason for pause. The storeowner seemed to know a lot about the case. Would he recognize him from the descriptions being circulated? Make the connection? He'd moved on to the next town to avoid being found out, and to keep the boys safe from those still searching for them. But had he gone far enough?

"I mean, just leaving your kids like that—"

"Maybe whoever left them didn't have a choice. Maybe they were doing what they thought best."

The storeowner shrugged. "Yeah. Maybe."

Another customer arrived at the counter. Paul, with his coffee and paper, headed out.

In his car, he spread Wednesday's edition out across his steering wheel. With only a hint of daybreak available, he switched on the overhead dome light so he could easily see.

Last week's update on the hearing indicated the judge might hand down a decision soon. It couldn't happen soon enough for Paul, eager to have some direction.

The boys were no longer safe in his custody. Somehow he'd been found out. The same car with the same driver had been following him for weeks. He'd managed to lose whoever it was each time but he didn't know how long his luck would hold out. Tucking the boys away at Sunny Brook until a better plan presented itself seemed the thing to do.

He finagled around with paperwork to legitimize his claim of guardianship and presented that to Mary. In his correspondence with her he claimed he'd lost his job and could no longer adequately care for the boys. She agreed to take them in at Sunny Brook temporarily. It all looked like it might work. Then Mik and Jeri ran off. Paul witnessed what took place in the parking lot that night. Stared in horror as it played out. From where he stood just outside his car on the side of the road, on the far side of the parking lot, he'd had no hope of being heard if he yelled out a warning to the officers.

He understood the reason for a hearing. The one witness, though drunk, conveyed intent. If the boys purposefully killed the officers then justice needed to be served. Yet he felt responsible and thanks to the storeowner, he now felt worse about not being able to do anything to help the boys.

He'd been able to do one thing though. He'd found the knife Jeri used to cut the cord to the drink machine. The blade glinted light from his flashlight beam when he played it around the area near the outlet. Somehow the police didn't find it. *But what was Jeri doing with my knife anyway?* Neither boy claimed to know where it was when it went missing the week before.

At least he had it now, which meant it would be more difficult to prove that either boy electrocuted the officers, intentionally or not.

He flipped through the pages, scoured each one and finally found the article on the hearing. He held his breath but exhaled relief when he saw the headline: "Seven-year-olds found not guilty."

Now, to catch up with the recent contact he'd made. He needed to know what place the judge might send the boys to, if he chose that option.

* * *

Two days after the trial, Judge Robert Kirkland stared at the official forms in front of him; bifocals perched on the end of his nose. He presently stared at a particular form that, with his signature, would send one of the boys off to Greenfield, the local mental hospital. Sam Hawkins, the clinical psychologist assigned to the group home where he'd placed the boys, recommended the action based on Jeri's self-destructive behavior. Over a forty-eight hour period, Sam had been called to the group home twice to evaluate. His conclusion: the boy was a danger to himself if left alone.

In spite of this and with a tainted bias based on documentaries he'd seen of past abuses of these institutions, Kirkland never easily sent any child to a mental institution. He removed his glasses, rubbed the bridge of his nose, then picked up the phone to call Sam.

"I was expecting to hear from you, Robert," Sam said when he answered.

"Then you know why I'm calling."

"Well it isn't hunting season yet so I pretty much figured."

83

The judge glanced at the wall-mounted deer antlers that hung between two tall bookcases; his trophy from last season's hunting with Sam. He used the antlers for a coat-and-robe-rack.

"I wish it was about something so trivial. So talk to me. What's going on with the boy?"

"The house-parents aren't equipped to deal with him. On four separate occasions they've walked in on him attempting to commit suicide—"

"Suicide? He's seven. What would he know about suicide? What's he grown up around?"

"Without any more information on his past I can't really say. I do know that after the first attempt they kept him close, yet he somehow managed to get out of their sight long enough to try again. The last time, he almost took his brother out."

"What are you saying? He tried to kill his brother?"

"No one knows for sure. I just know that when the staff walked in on him, the brother was on the floor unconscious. Jeri had already exposed the wires of a nearby cord with something sharp he'd found, and was leaning forward to touch him with it."

Robert sat numb from what he'd heard.

"You still there?"

"Did I make some sort of mistake?" Robert said. "*Is that* boy responsible for the death of those two officers?"

"You considered all the evidence. All the facts. This boy just needs specialized help that the group home can't provide."

"And you think sending him to Greenfield will help him?"

"I can't predict the future on that. And I know how you feel about institutionalizing any child, but I don't see any way around it."

Robert sighed deep. "All right then. I'll sign this form and get it faxed on over."

"I've got one other request if you don't mind hearing it."

"Sure. What is it?"

"I'd like to take Jeri's brother Mik. After he came around last night—from whatever happened to him, he had no memory of anything. He'd gone from easy to work with to being confused and angry. I don't want to see him go to Greenfield. I'm pretty sure I can save that one."

Robert chuckled lightly. "We're two of kind, you and I. We never get tired of helping the strays. I'll send that paperwork behind this fax."

* * *

The anesthesiologist stood nearby in case any problems arose. The ECT operator adjusted the strap so the electrodes lined up properly on the young patient's head. Because the patient was smaller than an adult, things had to be adjusted.

"Just relax," one attendant said as he tightened the straps on the straitjacket. "Just want to make sure you don't move."

"Nice that he has no hair," another said. "Sure makes positioning the electrodes easier. But what is that disk on the back of his neck? That's just weird."

"Don't you mean weirder?" said the first attendant who'd spoken.

Heavy eyelids threatened to close. The anesthesiologist nodded that it was safe to proceed. The muscle relaxant would keep any convulsions from being too violent. The machine, set to release 100 volts in one-second intervals, hummed to life at the flip of a switch.

But instead of delivering the current in intervals, the indicator showed that the machine must have malfunctioned: It had dumped the entire electrical load all at once. Frantic, they yanked at the electrodes, fought at the constraints of the straitjacket to free the boy, to see if he was all right. Two fingers went to his neck.

"I've got a pulse," someone said.

The boy's eyes shot open. "More," he said, uttering the first word since he'd been admitted the day before. "Need more juice."

"I'm pretty sure that would kill you," a nearby assistant offered.

At that response, Jeri pushed up off the table, moved through those standing around it to get to the ECT machine. He flipped the switch he'd seen the other man switch a moment ago, and held one of the electrodes against his head. With his free hand, he held out an open palm.

"What's he doing?" one attendant said, and moved toward him to take the electrode away. Jeri directed a concentrated surge of electricity in that man's direction, and the next one who approached. By the time it dawned on them to flip the breaker to the room, Jeri had absorbed enough current to kill a man four times his size.

* * *

Paul sat in a back booth of a local eatery, his contact having called ten minutes ago to tell him to meet him here. Nervous, he glanced at his watch after taking a seat. It was 5:07 in the afternoon. His contact wasn't exactly late, but he was eager for news. He needed every bit of information he could get to devise a plan to get the boys back.

Five minutes later, his contact found him in the back booth. As he slid into his seat, he pulled out an envelope and placed it on the table between them. "I can't take your money," he said.

Paul looked and found all the money inside. "You get half whether you have good information or not. That was the deal." He thought for a moment. "Please don't tell me you found nothing."

"I'm sorry. I tried. I did find the home they were sent to, but they were no longer there. And absolutely no one would divulge where they'd gone. The judge has done a real good job hiding these boys. Maybe he did it for their own safety. I don't know. But yeah, I'm sorry. I can tell you're upset about it. Sorry I couldn't help."

The man got up. Paul watched his back as he disappeared out the door and into the parking lot, a sick feeling in the pit of his stomach. Of all the outcomes he'd prepared for, a complete dead-end wasn't one of them. For the next ten minutes, he sat and tried to wrap his mind around what had just happened. Tried to come to terms with the facts. Thanks to his carelessness, an entity from God-knew-where was loose in society. An entity that had already killed two men. How many more would die?

"God help us all," he muttered, called the waitress over, ordered a cup of coffee, and tried to think of his next step.

Chapter 15

He sat on his bed in a windowless room in the hospital's subbasement, his back against one of four cement walls. An electrical wire ran out of a hole he'd created with a metal bedframe leg so many years ago. The hole had been necessary to get to the wiring. There were no electrical outlets in his room, those being considered dangerous to someone like him.

Bared wire taped to the round metal disk just under his hairline, which in this case merely separated skin from skin as there was no body hair to speak of, he sat with arms pulled tight around him.

Twenty years ago, before they banished him to the dungeons of Greenfield Mental Hospital, writing him off as incurable, they'd secured his arms with a straitjacket before submitting him to electric shock treatment. The shock treatment had saved his life, if not in the way they intended, or expected. He'd grown accustomed to the position, and even drew comfort from it while he charged.

He learned to draw current slowly during those earlier years so as not to alarm the attendants into ending his daily treatment early if he took all the current in at once, as he'd done the first time. He drew the current slowly, but a little faster than usual because today, he had a schedule to keep. Today he had to leave.

* * *

Monty's low baritone hum preceded him as he pushed the food cart along and down the hall, shuffling about his business as he routinely delivered dinner trays and meds to those patients housed on the hospital's basement level, those deemed criminally insane and too dangerous to be housed with the others. Their behavior controlled by a variety of antipsychotic drugs, depending on their condition, Monty likened them to zombies. Mute, will-less individuals, provided they took their medication. And of course that was part of his job, to make sure they took it.

Monty made his way around the first corner, systematically placing trays in a slot just beneath the small barred window in each heavy locked door after each patient had downed their pills. He'd then move onto the next cell.

The patient at the end of his route had been with them the longest and truth be told, Monty had developed a bit of a soft spot for him. Dark hands gripped the cart's push-bar as he moved along to finish up his shift for the day. He belched laughter upon spotting his favorite patient grinning out at him, the only patient he had to show any emotion. Yet the grin seemed much wider today. Appeared a little like a grimace.

"If I didn't know better, I'd think you were up to something," Monty said while he set a tiny paper cup with pills and a larger one with water down on the slot in the door, but didn't watch like he did with the other patients. He knew this patient would comply. He always did. He turned instead to get the food tray.

"Yeah, it's like you're planning something," he repeated, chuckling as he straightened.

Upon turning back toward the door, his eyes widened with fear. Loose items on the tray rattled as he shook. He glanced at the patient, the closed door the patient now stood in front of, and then back to the patient. "H-how did you get out? How the hell did you get out?"

No words followed. Instead, an arm extended out. Monty dropped the tray he held and backed up, bumping into the food cart behind him. "You—you get back in there," he tried. "I won't tell anybody. You just get back in there." As he backed away the young man stood his ground, arm extended.

Monty slid along the wall and almost made it to the elevator. He reached out to hit the call button, but was caught up in a force so strong he couldn't move.

An overload of current raced through his body. Muscles convulsed, contracting involuntarily. Seconds later he collapsed in a heap onto the tile floor.

Time passed, and a stiff Monty pulled his arm over and lifted his head to stare at his watch. The second hand no longer moved. He pushed himself up, wondering why he was so sore, and stared at a clock on the wall, did the math and realized he'd been on the tile floor for about an hour. *Gotta check that blood sugar more often,* he thought. Being diabetic had its drawbacks.

He looked at the dinner cart to see what he needed to do to finish his rounds. The last patient's tray wasn't on there. He looked over at the door and saw it sitting in the slot. He stared through the small observation window and spoke. "You didn't eat your dessert. You sure you're all done?" He never asked any of the other patients this. And of course this patient never spoke, so he'd have to watch his head for a nod one way or the other.

Electric Angel

"Okay then," he said, turned away from the window. "I guess I'll see you in the morning. Sweet dreams." He pushed the cart along and disappeared into the elevator unbothered that he'd just spoken to a patient that wasn't there.

* * *

At 9:27 P.M., twenty-four-year-old Luis Sanchez sped along familiar streets in the lower east side of Newark, carelessly maneuvering a stolen SUV. With his right hand, Luis rifled through the contents of the purse on the seat beside him. Then just picked up and dumped it, his crude, gold-grilled smile glinting light from the dashboard readout. He snatched up the cell phone he saw and dialed.

"Yo *hombre*. I'm almost there. I'm comin' around the back way. Be watching." He ended the call and moved to put the phone down when a jolt of electricity shot up his arm. His muscles contracted in response and no matter how hard he tried, he couldn't turn the device loose. His fingers remained clamped around it.

Sparks arced across his grills. Muscles contracted and the SUV veered erratically off the road. With no one to control it, the big vehicle slammed head-on into a utility pole. The snapped pole fell and dropped live wires. One fell across the stolen SUV. Another fell into a blood-filled puddle beyond where a man lay, felled by a shotgun blast.

While Luis was sending a long-overdue and too-late final prayer to God, emergency vehicles sped along to the scene: an ambulance and two squad cars, because gangs targeted unescorted emergency vehicles. Two paramedics had been killed a month before on an official call. They no longer took chances.

Wrecked vehicle in sight, the first squad car stopped. It took only seconds for the officers to figure out what had happened: A utility pole had snapped from the force of the SUV plowing into it. Lines were down, though, and they were live. Keying his radio, one officer radioed in. "Somebody get Anderson Electric on the horn. We need them to cut the power. We've got a couple lines down."

"Looks like the driver's toast," one paramedic observed. Wispy white smoke hung close to the roof inside the wrecked SUV's cabin. The stiff form lay awkwardly across the steering wheel.

A voice rang out from the other side of a broken-down fence that two of the officers had gone around. "Make that two victims. We've got another man down over here. But I'm not sure it's related to the wreck. Looks like he's been shot. I'm guessing he's dead since one of those downed wires is laying across him."

"Gangs," an officer stated, checked his weapon with his hand. Seconds later, a shot rang out. Everyone scurried for cover or hit the ground. No second shot followed.

"Did anybody see where that shot came from?"

There was the sound of surprised laughter from the back side of the fence. "The guy in the puddle. I don't think he's dead."

An officer with a flashlight moved around the fence. "Yeah, and he's got a gun." Then, just beyond that, the light caught something bouncing back the flashlight's beam. A badge. "And he's one of ours."

"His firing the weapon doesn't mean he's alive," one paramedic offered. "Could just be an involuntary reaction from all that voltage going through him."

The officer with the flashlight worked off that theory. "Hey, buddy," he called out. "If you fired that gun on purpose, can you fire it again?"

A second shot rang out.

"Shit, he's alive." The officer who'd called in to have Anderson Electric notified to cut the power keyed the radio again. "What's taking Anderson Electric so damn long? We need the power cut now. We've got an officer down."

* * *

Fritz Anderson deplored black-tie affairs. Avoided them whenever he could. To be the guest of honor at this one didn't change his opinion. Perhaps something catastrophic would happen and the event cancelled. An hour into the event, Fritz decided to push that line of thinking aside. Not even a catastrophe could make up for the lost time spent here. He was simply stuck with his misery.

Adrift in a sea of tables clad in white, pristine tablecloths that touched the floor, Fritz settled in to endure the rest of the evening. "I'm sorry," he said, realized he'd missed half of what the mayor just said to him. "You were saying?"

"I said how did you do it? How did you come in with such a lowball bid that no one else could even compete? I have to tell you, it's going to be interesting to see how you pull it off. With such a low bid, Anderson Electric can't possibly stand to make any money. If the city weren't in such dire need of your gratitude, I'd probably launch a full scale investigation." The mayor punctuated that comment with a light-hearted, well-meaning laugh.

Gratitude indeed. Fritz forced a smile nonetheless. "Anything to help the community." He braved a slightly sarcastic tone that was lost in the moment.

"Those people deserve so much more than what they're getting right now," the mayor continued. "I'm sure you saw that yourself after our visit last month."

Fritz recalled the squalor and disrepair, the dark corners of unlit ground-floor lobbies where tenants should've felt

93

safe, the rank smell of urine in dark elevators. More than that, he recalled having to purchase new shoes due to stepping into the source of the pungent odor.

The mayor had arranged the trip to the projects to encourage low bids. Fritz already had his bid in mind however, though for different reasons, and could've forgone the formalities of visiting the folks who were in such dire need of free services.

"Yes," he said after a moment. "I'm so happy to help the city provide for them."

A tap on his shoulder had Fritz turning. One of his entourage interrupted. "You have a call," the assistant said, held out a cell phone.

Fritz scowled. "Can you not see I'm busy?" All while he hoped the call was urgent enough to take him away from this nightmare early.

"No, no," the mayor insisted, waved his free hand in front of him. "Go take care of business, and congratulations again on winning the bid."

Fritz stood, walked with his man until they stood outside and away from any ears that might overhear.

"It's Bill," the man who'd pulled him away said, handing him the cell.

"Bill?" Ironic. Bill was project engineer for the very substation supplying the load to the projects he'd won the bid on. He pressed the phone to his ear. "This is Fritz. Is there a problem?"

"We have a request from the police to cut the power where an SUV wrecked and snapped a pole."

"And you called me why?"

"Because … no one can get near the controls. There's like a force field or something. It's electrical. I thought you might want to know. The police are getting anxious. They need the power cut, and I'm concerned they might send someone if we can't cut the power soon."

Fritz had prepared for this scenario on some level. "Cut the load coming into the station."

"But sir, that would take down the entire grid—"

"Are you questioning me? Cut the power. Make the adjustments, then bring the station back online with manual controls. I'll be there as soon as I can get there."

* * *

The dropped lines stopped sparking as soon as Anderson Electric had cut the power. It shouldn't have gotten darker all around them though. All eyes went to the skyline.

"Son of a bitch," someone muttered. "They've cut the power to everything."

Considering that light was the only deterrent against crime in this area, they knew they had to get out, and soon, or possibly not make it out alive.

Chapter 16

The stiff body of Luis Sanchez lay in the ambulance in a body bag. Medics worked feverishly to save the other man, whom they'd carefully turned over onto his back.

"Anybody have a chest they can spare?" one man asked, viewing the torn flesh. Pitted and bloody from shotgun pellet entry wounds, the chest resembled raw hamburger meat.

"Nice to know what we're up against," one of the officers muttered, "should we come under fire."

The paramedic working with the patient rattled off vital signs for his partner to hear. "Pulse 115, blood pressure 155 over 72." Suddenly his voice changed to a more urgent one. "Wait, I've lost his pulse." A moment later, "He's coding."

The second paramedic, standing in the back of the ambulance after he'd pulled it over close to the puddle, grabbed the portable defibrillator and jumped down to assist. Set up in seconds, and having handed the paddles over to his partner, he waited for the machine to charge to the desired level. "Okay," he said once it peaked.

"Clear" the other paramedic called out before he pressed the button to discharge the current to shock the heart. Yet the machine didn't seem to operate correctly. The charge seemed to fizzle to nothing. The patient lay still, seemingly unaffected. And then the first paramedic reported that the battery showed as being dead when it carried a full charge just moments ago.

Concerned for the patient now, the paramedic holding the paddles rushed to check for a pulse … and found one. "He's one lucky bastard. There's a pulse. Let's get him in the ambulance before something else goes wrong."

En route to the hospital, the patient hovered dangerously on the edge of dysrhythmia. Once at the emergency room entrance, the waiting trauma team took over.

The lead team member directed as the gurney was pushed along and the patient was fast-tracked through screening procedures. Within a few minutes of his arrival, he was moved into a treatment room. Scissors cut at the patient's torn and bloody shirt. A doctor with a magnifying visor began to pick out metal fragments near the surface of the skin. An ultrasound was clipped up so the lead team member could assess the damage. There was no pericardial fluid, a good sign that none of the shrapnel had reached his heart. A chest X-ray beside it revealed multiple shotgun pellets. The lead team member ordered a CT scan to further define the extent of the injuries.

Blood-matted hair from a laceration that seemed to stretch around to the back of his head had the lead team member adding, "He'll need stitches to close up that wound." A nurse moved in to comply. She reached for and picked up an electric razor lying atop a stainless-steel medical tray. She switched it on and brought the razor in close. Without warning and much to the nurse's surprise, the patient's eyes sprang open and in a Michael Myers fashion, an arm shot up. Fingers wrapped the nurse's wrist in a viselike grip and spittle sprayed from the patient's mouth as he fought sedation to speak. "Get back or I swear to God, I'll snap her wrist."

No one moved. He tightened his grip at their noncompliance. The nurse whimpered and her hand turned even whiter. The razor she held fell to the floor, where it skittered across the tile until it met with a nearby wall. The force of impact dislodged the battery, silencing the runaway razor.

"*Now!*" the patient bellowed. Those seemingly rooted to the floor stumbled over their own feet to back away.

The nurse breathed relief. She wasn't free, but at least he'd loosened his hold a little.

"So what do you want?" the team leader asked. "We need to proceed."

"Ghost."

Each confused face in the room searched the other before the patient added, "Find Ghost. Bring him here."

A young man closer to the back of the room took a stab at what those words might actually mean. "It must be his partner. I heard the cops that came in with the ambulance say he was a cop too. I'll go see if they might know who he's talking about. See if they can help locate this Ghost person."

Having watched and absorbed his share of horror movies in his day, he stopped short of pushing through the swinging double doors that led out and added, "Or Dr. Loomis."

* * *

The emergency room doors hissed open and then closed. An attendant at the information desk looked up. With a stern expression and a no-nonsense tone she asked, "Can I help you?"

He didn't carry much weight on his leptosomic frame and though his clothes fit, they hung loosely. Even with a belt, his jeans sagged low on hips that were barely there.

He was thin and pale, and bore a striking resemblance to one of his rocker idols Mick Jagger, a coincidence that served him well when it came to picking up women but not so well in this instance.

He pulled a badge from a back pants pocket and showed it to the woman behind the counter, whose expression didn't change much in spite of learning he was a police officer.

"I'm looking for my partner. They said he was here."

"Name?"

He squinted confusion. "My name? Charles Hawkins."

She looked up from the chart in front of her. "No, your partner's name. Why would it help to have your name?"

"Why would it help to have my partner's name? They told me he didn't have any ID on him."

"Well, without a name I can hardly help you find him."

"Just tell me where they took the patient they brought in with a shotgun blast to the chest."

"I'm sorry, but I have to have a name."

A young man in a lab coat appeared. He had slid around the corner and heard part of the conversation. "Did you say you were looking for your partner?"

"Yeah. He was shot. I was told they brought him here. I'm his partner, Charles. Charles Hawkins." He showed the badge once more. But the young man seemed more interested in the tips of the fingers that held it. More specifically, the letters tattooed on each one. "You're Ghost."

He'd tattooed the letters that spelled the word Ghost on the fingertip of each finger of his left hand. "Oh yeah," he said when he realized what the young man had seen. "I don't have any fingerprints. Long story. They call me Ghost."

Ghost followed where the young man led, entered the treatment room behind him, and paid attention when he said, "There he is."

On the gurney lay his partner, the muscles in his right arm tense, the fingers of his right hand clenched tightly around the frail wrist of a white-with-fright nurse. His chest looked like fresh road-kill and the doctors and nurses who should've been addressing the matter all stood as one in the shadows of the light focused over the work area.

"Can you get him to let her go so we can help him?"

He wasn't sure which one of them had spoken. There were ten of them and one nurse. Surely they had sedatives. He sighed at their inability to come up with a plan and headed over. "You're never going to get a date like that," he said as he leaned in close. A blur of activity followed and ended with the nurse being free and Ghost held captive. "Ease up," he said after being yanked down by his shirt and granted a front-row seat to the carnage that was his partner's chest.

"Tell them—not to cut my hair."

Ghost angled his eyes to find the lead doctor. "Did you hear that? He says don't cut his hair."

"But he needs stitches."

Ghost saw his partner's right arm shoot out, grab something off a nearby tray and then felt something sharp at his neck. He knew right away it was a scalpel. "Tell them," is what he heard just before he felt the sting of the blade being brought in closer.

"Unless you want another patient to tend to, I suggest you assure him you won't cut his hair."

"Yes, of course," the doctor rushed to say. "We don't have to cut his hair."

The arm holding Ghost fell limp, but he didn't pull away

100

until he heard the scalpel hit the tile floor. Those waiting to get back to work rushed past him.

"Do you need help with that?" one of them asked Ghost.

"Huh?"

The man pointed at his throat. "You're bleeding."

It wasn't until then that Ghost felt a wee trickle. He wiped with a hand. "Son of a bitch," he said as he stared at the traces of blood on his fingers. "He cut me."

"I can take care of that if you want me to."

"So can I," Ghost said, rattled. "Just point me to the nearest bathroom."

"Out that door and to your left."

Ghost walked off still rubbing at the cut, and wondering how he'd actually come that close to having his throat slit.

Chapter 17

Fritz rode in silence as he thought about what needed to be done to get the substation back online as quickly as possible. While he'd prepared for such a scenario, he hadn't expected one. Things had run so smoothly until now.

When the massive towers supporting the high-voltage lines came into view, he leaned forward. When the car slid to a stop in the dirt parking lot, he jumped out. Moved fast enough to avoid being caught up in the dust cloud he created. He found Bill exactly where he expected to find him—bent over a control panel as he kept an eye on things.

"I trust you have it contained," Fritz said while he walked toward a door that required a keypad code to get in. Decisive fingers stabbed out the sequence.

"Yes," Bill said. "It's safe to go in."

The containment area was a twelve-by-twelve metal-lined and thickly concreted square room that sat inside a much larger room. High-voltage wires ran in from the roof, and a viewing window occupied a wall near the only door. Normally the room was dark and void.

Presently, it glowed with the entity's presence.

Fritz strode over to peer inside. Pressed a button near a speaker grate and spoke. "Are we quite through playing games?"

The glow's intensity waned. The process of denying it energy had taken its toll. "I'm so very weak," a voice replied. A woman's voice. A voice Fritz knew to be Anna Chadwick's.

"What were you doing anyway?" he said. "What were you up to?"

"I—I'm sorry … won't happen again … energy … need energy."

"I don't know," Fritz countered. "I'm not sure you've suffered enough." From all indications, he understood that depriving the entity of much-needed electricity could elicit pain. Sudden drops in current seemed to bring extreme discomfort. "Perhaps wearing you down a little more will help you understand the importance of doing as you're told."

"I understand. Please … so weak."

He released the button he'd been holding down and headed out.

"Bring her back online," Fritz told Bill. "But monitor things closely for the next twenty-four hours. Reel her back in at the first sign of trouble." He looked back over his shoulder. "Oh, and I want a report on my desk in the morning concerning what happened. I want to know the exact time the outage occurred, the affected area, anything that can help me determine what she might be up to."

He pulled open the door that led out. "Keep me posted."

* * *

Ghost slumbered in a chair in the hospital room next to the bed where his partner lay, sprawled out like a rag doll tossed aside. Him, not his partner. He slept as best he could, one leg over an arm, head hanging over the back. He jerked awake when his partner stirred. His chair level with the bed, he sat up and moved to the edge of it.

"How you doing, Mik?"

Groggy eyes fluttered open. "How should I be doing? What happened?"

"You don't remember?"

Mik squinted at the ceiling. "I sort of remember ... they wanted to cut my hair ..."

"Yeah," Ghost said. Recalled the scalpel held against his throat and rubbed at his neck.

Mik glanced over at Ghost when he did this. "If you'd been more convincing about my request not to have my hair cut, I wouldn't have had to threaten to slice your throat open."

Ghost stopped rubbing at his neck. His eyes narrowed. "You better tell me you weren't aware of what you were doing when you took that scalpel and held it to my throat."

Mik shrugged. "Whatever you want to think."

But then, how would he know to say what he'd just confessed to unless he was in fact aware? "Asshole. You drew blood."

"I had to do something," Mik said, complacent. "They were about to cut my hair."

"And you were about to cut my throat."

"Don't be so dramatic. My hand slipped. That's all."

The quarter-sized implanted metal disk on the back of Mik's neck, just below the hairline, caused Ghost more grief than he cared to think about. Mik didn't want anyone else to know about it, and so as a young boy swore Ghost to secrecy when he revealed it to him. He wore his blonde hair long to hide it.

Ghost sank back in his chair. Pressed on to the other issue that had him concerned. "So what were you doing, Mik? Why did they find you where they found you? That part of town—it isn't even our jurisdiction. You'll be lucky if Cap doesn't put you on probation."

"I don't have to answer to him when I'm off duty."

"Yeah. That defense worked so well last time. And that's fine if you want to use that excuse again. But I want to know the truth. Why did you want to go there? And why did you go alone? I would've gone with you. At least you would've had some backup."

"No offense, but with no gun, choosing you for backup hardly makes sense."

Ghost inherited dermatopathia pigmentosa reticularsis from someone in his family, but since he never knew either parent and was put up for adoption at birth, he didn't know who to blame. He did know that DPR robbed him of having fingerprints, which made life hell for him. After three years of attempts, he'd still not been able to pass a background check. Until such time, he worked the front desk and sometimes dispatched. Mik often held this over his head, but usually to avoid answering a question.

"Sticks and stones but I still want to know."

Mik let his head roll away from Ghost. "I don't know. Something … I just felt— I don't know."

Ghost nodded. It wasn't the first time Mik had ended up somewhere without any knowledge of why he went and sometimes even how he got there. "That's what I thought. Just wanted to make sure I guess."

Mik turned his head back toward Ghost. "You'll help me think of something to tell Cap, right? I can't take another suspension."

"I always do, don't I?"

Mik's eyelids slid shut then, and Ghost watched as his friend slipped back into a drug-induced slumber. The clock on the wall read four in the morning. *Great*, Ghost thought.

I've got roughly three hours to come up with a story Cap won't be able to see straight through.

Chapter 18

The nametag pinned to the lapel of the hospital-issued lab coat read R. Trent. The young man who slipped into the coat entered the hospital morgue to begin his shift. Luis Sanchez's electrocuted body lay on the first gurney he passed. He paid little attention to it until he heard a cellphone ringtone that seemed to come from just inside the body bag that held the body. He took the few steps back to the gurney and unzipped the zipper. There, in the right hand, was the phone in question.

Idly wondering why it had been left with the corpse, he attempted to take it to bag it and let his supervisor know, but the fingers were securely wrapped around it. He therefore leaned to see if he could respond to the call that way. He managed to press the call button, said hello, then shot up from where he leaned when the phone sputtered, sparked and exploded. It then fell from the hand in shattered, melted pieces.

* * *

Fritz sat behind his desk the next morning and ignored his coffee. He scrutinized every inch of the report Bill sent him. Looked for anything that might help him understand just what happened the night before while he attended the gala in his honor. Why did the entity not automatically cut power to the damaged grid, and why did it override the manual controls?

Perhaps it had something to do with the accident itself. Since nothing else made sense, Fritz decided to do a little investigating. Perhaps knowing more about the accident would settle the matter.

A little before lunch, he was bothered with a call from the chief of police, routed to him by the mayor. So much for putting it off. He had to take the call. He listened with little interest as the police chief ranted about how the safety of his officers was compromised and how they needed to know about such matters *before* they happened.

"Yes, I understand," Fritz answered, attempted to sound fully chastised. "It was a horrible mistake, and I've taken care so it won't happen in the future. However, wasn't the individual already dead when your men got there? Of course that doesn't excuse having to take the entire grid down, but perhaps if we'd had a little more time to fix things—"

Fritz raised his brows at the response, flipped back through Bill's report to see where the police had called back to say a man was alive: an officer. "Oh yes, I see that now. I apologize. The downed wires must've kept rescuers from getting to him."

The news from the chief that one of the downed wires had actually fallen across the officer stunned Fritz. No one should've survived that. "Well that is miraculous. I'd certainly like to offer this man my apologies myself. What hospital did they take him to?"

Miraculous indeed, Fritz thought, and as soon as the conversation ended, he called the hospital. First to learn more about the man involved in the accident, and second to set up a meeting with this officer. A wicked smile played on his lips. Had this been an attempt by Anna to save her boys? He'd always thought she knew where they were. Perhaps he was about to find out something that proved him right after all these years.

* * *

Long slender fingers wrapped around the badge that lay just beyond the blood filled puddle. Curious, colorless eyes studied the item unintentionally left behind the night before in the rush to save the officer to which it belonged.

"Hey," a voice called out. "Turn around slowly and hold your hands out in front of you so we can see them."

He straightened, and did as asked. Faced the one officer who'd spoken, and now stood in front of him and three others who stopped a few feet back.

"What do you want with this?" the officer asked upon taking the badge.

"Mik," came the reply.

"Excuse me?"

"Mik."

The officer glanced over his shoulder at the others before he continued. "You know who this badge belongs to?"

Again, "Mik."

"Okay." The officer shrugged nonchalantly as he reached for cuffs attached to his belt. "If that's all you can give me I'm going to have to place you under arrest." And he read him his rights, then escorted the bald, eyebrow-less young man to the squad car and directed him to the back seat. He then called ahead on the radio. "We have someone in custody who might have been involved with the shooting last night. Where do I take him?"

Officer Redding of Precinct 4 responded. "Bring him to us. We want a crack at him first."

"That's not proper protocol," the patrol officer grinned as he spoke. "You guys gonna cover the paperwork?"

"We'll cover it. Just get him over here."

Chapter 19

With bandages wrapped tight, Mik could move with minimal pain. The pain had reduced everything to a tolerable dull ache. By late afternoon, his doctor could only shake his head at the dramatic improvement of his condition. "I've never seen anything like it, but I still think you should stay another twenty-four hours for observation. You almost died last night."

"Well you know what they say." Mik buttoned up the shirt. "'Almost' only counts in horseshoes and hand grenades."

"Just make sure and sign the release forms before you leave."

An hour later, Mik stood in front of Cap's desk and shoved those release forms over for Cap to see. "I'm cleared to go back to work."

Cap looked up from where he'd been writing, his clipped words indicative of his mood. His hot-blooded Italian temper simmered. "You expect me to put you back to work this soon. Go home."

"You don't have to put me on the streets. I'll just hang out around here. You're always saying you're shorthanded."

He didn't look up this time. "Do you know what I'm filling out? A report. Do you know why I'm filling it out?

111

Because of you. It's already taken me all morning and I've better things to do. The last thing I need is to have you hanging around possibly stirring up trouble."

He did look up then. "You're a good cop and I'm glad you're all right, but I just don't need the additional headache right now. Go home. Get some rest." His hand went back to writing.

Prepared to argue further, Mik drew a breath. But then he saw Redding eagerly motioning for him. He left Cap to his work.

Redding led him away from Cap's office before he revealed what he wanted.

"How're you feeling?"

"Like a truck hit me. But you didn't pull me out of there to discuss how I'm feeling. What's up?"

A twisted grin preceded Redding words. "They think they found the guy who shot you. We had them bring him here. We thought you might want to talk to him first."

Interest piqued, Mik replied, "Really?"

"Oh yes. We thought you could use the old interrogation room." Located at the end of a long hall, it had become a storage room of sorts for old files and other things no one needed or wanted to deal with. "Once you're done with the guy, we'll send him on his way—if there's anything left to send."

Mik's reputation preceded him. He rarely passed up the opportunity to "physically" interrogate anyone if he could get away with it. Cap had written up several reports about those incidents. In his present condition, still not completely healed of his injuries, he wasn't certain just how much damage he could inflict. Yet it wasn't in him to pass up the opportunity.

"So how's this going to work?"

"The same way it always works. Come on."

Redding led him to the room and told him to wait. "We'll have to bring him in the back way to get by Cap, so it might be a minute. But we'll leave him cuffed." Redding pulled the door closed and left.

Mik leaned against one of four walls to wait. Straightened when he heard subtle noises from out in the hall. Then the door opened, and a hooded-and-cuffed individual was led in. His attire: gray medical scrub shirt and matching pants with black flip-flops. *Interesting*, Mik thought. Nothing about the man before him screamed gang member.

"We'll leave you girls alone," Redding quipped.

"Uncuff him," Mik said before Redding could get away.

"You sure about that."

"I wouldn't have said it if I wasn't sure."

Redding had the cuffs off in seconds, returned them to his belt. "We'll be just outside when you're done." Redding then pulled the door shut behind him.

The hooded suspect stood silent but turned with Mik when Mik circled him. Mik reached out and yanked the hood off.

"Whoa," he remarked, somewhat stunned at the lack of any facial hair, or hair of any kind. No eyebrows, no afternoon shadow. Then there were those clear, colorless eyes. "I was not expecting that. What's wrong with you?"

"Mik," came his response.

"So you know my name. Good. Then you'll know who kicked your ass."

As though speech were a challenge for him, he continued. "I know you. I know all about you." He reached out with his right arm. "Touch me and you'll understand."

113

Mik batted the arm away, but voiced surprise at what felt like an electrical shock that left him rubbing his arm. "What the hell?"

"Just touch me."

The door flew open and Cap bellowed loud enough for anyone around to hear, "What's going on?"

"I can explain," Redding started, having raced toward the sound of Cap's voice.

"Am I talking to you?"

"No sir." Redding shrank back.

"I'd be an idiot not to know what's going on, since this isn't the first time something like this has happened." Cap turned to face Mik. "What part of 'Go home' didn't you understand? Fifth Precinct just called. The gang member that shot you last night was picked up with your wallet still on him. This man is innocent."

Cap addressed Redding then. "Make sure he finds his way safely out of this building. The last thing I need is more paperwork to fill out." Then back to Mik. "Hawkins, you're on suspension until further notice."

From where he'd been standing just behind Cap, Ghost took a step forward. Mik couldn't afford too many more suspensions, and he was hell to live with when he was on one. Since they shared an apartment, Ghost said, "He didn't do anything."

"Exactly," Cap snapped. "I told him to go home and he didn't. And since you're his transportation, you're suspended too."

"What?"

"You heard me. And if he shows back up here today, then the both of you can find work elsewhere."

* * *

Twenty years had passed. Reginald Palmer had moved on with life. Oh, Reg made a few attempts in the years that followed to find the boys, but none of his searches yielded anything. They might as well have vanished off the planet.

Therefore, when he recognized the officer a local newscaster reported on that evening, he very nearly choked on his late dinner. Twenty years, and Mik still looked the same, more or less. Reg listened closely. Copied down the name of the hospital, and since it was late, made plans to visit the following day.

He arrived at the hospital in time for visiting hours and to make sure Mik had been moved to a room. "I'm here to see Mik Hawkins," he told the woman staffing the information desk, then waited while the woman pecked at a keyboard.

"He's already been released."

Reg squinted confusion. "Wasn't he in serious condition last night?"

"I can't divulge any of that information."

Of course you can't, he thought. But then he'd just been thinking aloud anyway.

"Guess I should've checked before I came," he said. "Thank you anyway."

As he left, his mind screamed for answers. How does anyone who sustained a shotgun blast to the chest at close range manage to walk out of the hospital less than twelve hours later?

* * *

Fritz shrank back into the shadows before Reg could see him. Then he followed at a safe distance. When Reg exited to the parking lot, Fritz readied the camera on his cell. When Reg pulled up to pay the parking fee at the station, Fritz snapped a picture of his license tag. He then forwarded it and made a call. "Track it, find out where he lives and search his home. You know what to look for."

Chapter 20

Reg had an appointment with a client. He left the hospital and drove the short distance over. Results of the audit tucked under an arm, he stepped out of his parked car and entered their office to discuss the results. Distracted, he worked to wrap the matter up quickly. After a brief summary and explanation on how they should proceed he was headed home, determined to start his search for Mik now that he knew he was still alive. He pulled into his driveway, stepped out of his car and noticed his back door standing open. He knew he'd locked it.

He saw a baseball bat, left by a neighbor's child. He picked it up, listened for noises as he approached his back door and moved in cautiously. But who would rob anyone in broad daylight?

Turning the corner into the kitchen, he could see the room had been turned upside down. Drawers and cabinets yanked open and left that way; an entire pack of paper napkins ripped open and strewn across the room; the refrigerator and freezer doors wide open. Whoever had broken in had definitely been looking for something. *But what?*

He moved into the living room and found that room in shambles as well. He turned to his right, expecting the same, but his office was intact. Not one thing out of place.

117

His first thought was one of relief. His second thought had him racing into the room as he recalled what he'd left laying out.

"Oh my God," he said while he looked feverishly around, tried to recall if maybe he'd put the file up. "Please, no." He pulled the drawer open where he kept the file when not in use but didn't see it. Certain now of what had been taken, he sank into the chair behind his desk. Tried to convince himself there was nothing in the file that would really change things or compromise anyone's safety. He'd just about done it too, until he recalled that Zachary's current address was in that file. The realization told him what he had to do next.

* * *

Zachary parked in his assigned spot in front of his apartment and walked over to the mail kiosk to retrieve his mail. The neighbor who usually picked up his mail at the same time broke from the usual routine of just nodding. "I see you have guests this evening."

Zachary, assuming the neighbor saw something he'd missed, glanced back over his shoulder but saw nothing to suggest he might have visitors. "Why would you think that?"

"Well, three men showed up a while ago and asked if that was your apartment. Said they were old friends paying a visit. They said you told them to go on in but they wanted to make sure they had the right apartment."

Zachary wondered if his face reflected his ire, decided it didn't matter if it did. This man had just told complete strangers where he lived.

Apparently his look didn't show his confounded amazement. "They went on in," the neighbor said.

The neighbor turned then and walked off with his mail. Zachary turned as well and pretended to be studying his. He looked over at his top-floor apartment just in time to see a glint of light at the window. He had no idea it was a gun until the ping of metal hitting metal very near to where he stood told him it had to be. Of course he could be wrong but either way, running seemed the logical thing to do.

He took off back up the road that led in, heard a car engine race and then tires squeal. He wasn't in bad shape for a man his age, yet he knew he couldn't outrun a car, and getting lucky at dodging bullets seemed a matter of odds he didn't care to take a chance on. Instead, he darted off the road and down an embankment where no car could follow.

There was a road that ran behind the apartments and that's where he headed. Maybe a student or faculty member from the university would see him and offer help.

He couldn't imagine his luck when a car pulled up beside him and stopped.

"Get in," the man said. Zachary took a second to see if he recognized the driver. He didn't, though there was something oddly familiar about him. At any rate, the man didn't have a gun that he could see and seemed to want to help. He got in with seconds to spare; the thugs swung their car around the corner as he was closing his door.

"You know this area better than me," the driver said. "What's the best way to go to lose these guys?"

The man was a stranger to the area. Zachary would have to ask him about that later. "There's an intersection coming up. Take a left there."

The driver did as instructed.

"Go down two blocks then take another left. About a half mile down that road are some train tracks. In roughly four minutes a train will be coming through." Several students often used that train as an excuse for being late for his lab. "We need to be on the other side of those tracks before then. It's a long train. Takes about five minutes for it to clear the tracks."

The driver followed Zachary's directions to the letter. The thugs had fallen behind. The train rapidly approached the crossing but would those following see it in time to speed up and make it across too?

They hit the tracks doing seventy. Both Zachary and the driver each watched their side-view mirrors closely once on the other side. The car pursuing them fishtailed, then the train passing blocked their view.

Chapter 21

Both men sighed relief that the thugs had been caught by the train. "Head for that farm road up ahead," Zachary said, and pointed. "But drive in the grass beside it. It hasn't rained in about a week and with no wind, the dust cloud we'd create would hang in the air. There's a good chance anyone passing would see it."

About a quarter of a mile down that dirt road sat a barn. The man drove his car behind it and parked.

Zachary turned to face the driver. "Thanks for helping me out back there."

The driver shrugged "No problem. I'm just glad we lost them."

The way he said the words, the inflection, his tone— "My God Reg, is that you?"

"It's been a long time, hasn't it?"

A whirlwind of emotion forced Zachary's entire body, including his face, to go numb. What his expression couldn't portray, his actions did. He shoved the door of the car open hard and slammed it shut. He walked fast toward an open pasture and then he just stopped.

Reg caught up and stopped behind him. "Please let me explain."

"I don't want to hear anything you have to say."

"I understand. I do. But you have to listen to me."

Zachary turned to face him. "The last time I listened to you ... you betrayed me. I lost my family. I lost everything."

"I tried to get the boys back to you but something happened and I couldn't. But I think I can help you find them now."

Zachary stiffened and replied, his words cold and hard, "I'm not interested."

"You're lying," Reg challenged. "Hand me your wallet and I'll prove it."

Zachary hesitated, but the dangling carrot of finding out what happened to his children was too tempting. He handed over the wallet. Reg flipped through the contents. "Here," he said, held the wallet open. Directed a finger at a photo. "If you weren't interested, you wouldn't be carrying this around with you. This photo of your boys—the one I sent you along with that letter some twenty years ago."

"So you *were* the one who sent that."

"Yes. And there's quite a story to go along with it, but this isn't the place to tell you about it."

Zachary had to know. "So ... so how are they?"

The question seemed to throw Reg, then he said, "That's right, how would you know what happened? You couldn't possibly ... I lost them, Zachary. It's part of that story."

Zachary took the wallet back and returned it to his pocket. You can't blame me for feeling the way I do about you."

"I don't blame you. I can imagine how much you must hate me."

"Why were those men in my apartment after me? Was it the same bunch who helped you take the boys and Anna? What did they want?"

Electric Angel

"I'm afraid Fritz might have sent them."

Zachary recoiled at hearing the name.

"I know. It's hard for me to take too. After all these years."

"He took Anna that night."

Reg nodded. "I suspected as much. After I learned the boys had found a way to communicate with her, I realized she was still around. I think Fritz is using her, forcing her to help him. But none of that has anything to do with why those guys were after you. I'm afraid that was my fault. After all these years, I let my guard down." Reg looked around the pasture, saw no dust clouds coming in their direction. "But could we talk about this somewhere else?"

The sun was setting. Reg swatted at an insect that lit on his neck. Zachary nodded. "Sure. You can tell me that story along the way."

* * *

Sam Hawkins coughed and wheezed. Spit blood and phlegm into a kidney-shaped basin the nurse held. Mik and Ghost stopped in the doorway of the hospital room, hidden from view for the moment by a half-drawn curtain. Sam had spent the better part of the past year in the hospital with lung cancer. And his dementia had progressed to the point where sometimes he didn't recognize anyone.

Coughing spasm over, Sam barked at the nurse, "You think I can't put my own oxygen mask back on? I'm not an invalid."

Ghost attempted once more to talk Mik out of this visit. They'd seen Sam less than two weeks ago. "We can still leave. He hasn't seen us yet."

But the nurse had. "You have visitors," she chirped. Ghost grumbled a curse word.

"I don't want visitors," Sam growled.

123

"Hey Sam," Mik said, forced a smile. Ignored Ghost.

"What do you two want? And when was the last time you two came to visit anyway?"

"Two weeks ago," Ghost offered, though Sam rarely recalled.

"I need to talk to you about something," Mik told him.

Sam looked up from where he sat on the edge of the bed, drew several deep breaths through his oxygen mask. "What if I don't feel like talking?"

"Then I'll talk and you can listen. It's real important, Sam."

Ghost braced for the next outburst but had to raise a brow when Sam said, "Sure. What is it, son?"

Though he and Mik had been warned, Ghost gawked at the change that seemed to come over Sam. The doctors said there would be instances where Sam could push past his dementia to appear as they recalled him before the disease took over. Yet Ghost had never experienced this. Mik geared up to take advantage and carefully asked his question, the question that came to him shortly after the incident in the interrogation room, shortly after the shock he received from the supposed suspect that revealed he might indeed have a sibling he'd not been told of.

"Do I have a brother that you're aware of and maybe didn't tell me about?"

"Yes," Sam said without hesitation. "And I'm sorry I didn't say something to you sooner—you know, when you were older and could understand about such things. He's your twin actually, but he's … very different. We felt it best to put him in a place where he could get the help he needed." Sam stood, extended an arm out toward Mik. "If you'll just touch me … take my hand—you'll understand. Just touch me."

124

Having heard those same words, those exact same words not over two hours ago, Mik took a step back.

Sam took another step forward. "Just take my hand, please." The next step Sam took had the cord to the oxygen machine flying out of the wall outlet. He began gasping and calling out for the nurse.

Ghost ran past Mik to assist Sam. Mik stood and stared and then sprinted toward the hall. The hiss of an elevator's doors sliding shut had him looking. The bald passenger had him sprinting once again. But the doors closed before he could force them back open.

He'd take the stairs instead but he was on the fourth floor so he had to move fast.

Ghost saw him enter the stairwell and followed after. He reached the lobby shortly after Mik had.

"What's going on," he asked, coming up behind Mik. Then he saw the taxi pull away with its bald passenger. "Oh, him. He gets around doesn't he?"

* * *

Fritz slammed a fist onto the top of his desk when he got word that the goons he'd sent to ambush Zachary torched the apartment. He couldn't afford such incompetence. He'd be lucky if local police didn't investigate. And if they were stupid enough to make that decision on their own, no telling what they'd tell the authorities if they were caught and questioned.

Fritz made a call. "Take them out," he hissed into his phone, "quickly and silently." He frowned at the words that followed and said, "If you think that action is too rash then perhaps I need to put someone else in charge."

A smirk replaced the frown. "That's what I thought. Now let me know the second the men are taken care of."

125

Fritz made another phone call. "Call Bill," he said to his secretary. "Tell him I'll be there shortly."

* * *

Bill nursed another cup of coffee. The report Fritz wanted from him kept him up until around three that morning. He'd napped a few hours, his head on his desk, yet couldn't seem to shake the cobwebs of fatigue. Now Fritz wanted him to pull the entity back into the containment chamber.

He gulped to finish the coffee, stood and walked over to the controls, adjusted the main dial to increase the level of current in the chamber until it exceeded the current coming into the station. He watched until the numbers indicated an even larger increase in current, but one not caused by anything he did. When the current stabilized, he shut the door to the containment room and put the substation on automatic. The entity contained, he headed back to his desk for some much-needed sleep.

Chapter 22

Fritz arrived around five-thirty. Bill still slept at his desk. Fritz went on without waking him. He could tell from the readings that Bill had successfully pulled the entity in. The glow from within the containment room confirmed this. Fritz walked over and pressed the appropriate button to open communications. "Hello Anna."

"Why do you have me here?" came the reply.

"Because I feel you're withholding information and I want to know why."

"I don't know what you're talking about."

He keyed in a code that gave him access to the level of current in the room. Access gained, he turned a dial, which lowered the level significantly. The entity made a noise as if in pain. To deny it electricity was like denying a human oxygen.

"It would go so much easier for you if you'd just tell the truth. If I get satisfactory answers, I increase the current. So, tell me why you wouldn't allow the power to be cut last night when Bill instructed you to do so?"

"I told you. It won't happen again."

"Yes. I know what you said. But that's not an answer. Now I want to know why it happened in the first place. Is this Mik Hawkins one of the two that were taken the night I found you?"

127

"I don't know who you're talking about."

He held a plastic bag the size of a sandwich bag up to the small observation window. The entity couldn't see the way a human could, but Fritz had learned that in some form, it possessed all five senses. "This is what's left of the cell phone found on the young man who crashed into the utility pole that brought those wires down. He was talking on it when he crashed the vehicle. He was driving a stolen SUV, and this was a stolen phone. Just about the time he was in the area, an officer by the name of Mik Hawkins encountered a gang. He was off duty and had no real reason for being where he ended up."

"Why are telling me this?"

"I'm not finished," Fritz stated. "I think Mik Hawkins was in the area because you summoned him. I think you were making an effort to communicate with him and hoped the bigger transformer nearby would facilitate this effort. However, you didn't plan on the gang, or on Mik Hawkins being shot. After that happened, you needed to help Mik.

"Luis Sanchez happened to be in the area, and was on a cell phone. You called that phone and sent a mind-blowing surge of electrical current. Even helped maneuver the vehicle into that pole. One of the wires fell across the SUV, electrocuting Luis and assuring he wouldn't talk. Another landed very near where Mik Hawkins lay in a puddle.

"How do I know all this?" He glanced at what was left of the cell and then back into the chamber. "Because I had the log for incoming calls checked," he said of the phone, "once I was told by a source just what happened at the hospital morgue. Why, I wondered, would a phone explode upon being answered? It wasn't in this shape," he said of the bag's contents, "until after the accident—when *you* called the hospital, to destroy any evidence. You did this on

128

purpose. The last two incoming calls came from right here at the substation. One came in about the time of the accident. The other came seconds before you obliterated the device. Don't cross me," he said, reduced the current once more. "I'll have Bill accommodate your release from the containment room once I feel you've had time to think about your actions."

He headed toward the door. "Oh, and thank you for leading me to Mik. No doubt he can lead me to the two young men I sought that night—provided he isn't one of the two."

* * *

Zachary agreed not to push Reg for answers until they got to the motel. Beyond that, he promised nothing.

From one of the two beds, perched on the edge and staring once again at that photo—the one in his wallet—he began. "So you took them."

Reg walked over. Lowered himself onto the bed across from Zachary. "Yes Zachary, I took them. I took your children. I had to do something."

"*We* were doing something," Zachary protested

"But *you* didn't know everything. Fritz was blackmailing me. Fritz knew everything, Zachary. All the visits I made to your place, all the conversations we had. Everything you didn't want anyone to know. He knew."

"How?"

Reg sighed. "My briefcase. When I wouldn't sell you out—he had it wired. He knew I took that briefcase everywhere I went."

A stunned, "My God" fell from Zachary's lips.

"Exactly how I felt when Fritz told me what he'd done. When I learned he wanted the boys, I did everything I could to make sure he didn't get them."

"You did everything but tell me."

"Fritz is dangerous. He controlled every move I made. The only hope I had was to keep him from finding out I was up to something. If he'd known, he would've moved quicker. He would've killed me, you, and anyone who got in his way."

Before Zachary could respond to that, Reg held up a hand, grabbed up the television remote next to him on the bed, as he'd turned the TV on before he sat but muted it. At seeing the "breaking news" banner that scrolled across the screen, he turned the volume up.

A man with a microphone bearing the station's call letters stood in front of the burned-out hull of an apartment unit that contained four individual apartments. "… foul play hasn't been ruled out," the newscaster reported, "since two men were found in the woods beyond the apartment. They had been shot execution style with single bullets to the head." He then added, "No one was injured in the fire."

Reg put the television on mute once more.

"That was my apartment," Zachary gasped.

"And you can rest assured Fritz had those two men killed because they didn't deliver. Didn't bring you to him."

In spite of his shock, that drew a curious look from Zachary. "And you said you knew why they came after me."

He let out a frustrated sigh. "I let my guard down. After all this time." That thought had him shaking his head. "They ran a story on the news last night about an officer who'd been shot. I recognized the face at once. It was Mik."

With that being the first time he'd referred to either of the boys by name, Reg explained. "I recalled that you said you wanted to use your grandfather's name, Mikhail."

Zachary acknowledged with a nod.

"I called him 'Mik' for short. Anyway, I knew he was the officer in question when they flashed his image up on the screen. Plus, he still goes by Mik. I made plans to go see him at the hospital the following day. But, by the time I got there, he'd already been released. A few hours later I returned home to find my back door standing open. A file I'd pulled out, but usually keep hidden, was the only thing missing. And Fritz would be the only one interested in the contents. It was the file I've been keeping on you and your whereabouts—so I'd know how to contact you if I ever found the boys."

Saying all of this didn't help any of it make sense so Reg wasn't surprised by Zachary's confused look. He geared up to try harder. "I came to your apartment to let you know that things had gone bad. I was a little late … or just in time depending on how you want to look at it."

Zachary's eyes glazed as he turned his attention back to the photo in his wallet. He'd rubbed his wrists raw that night trying to break free of the ropes that bound him to the chair. He'd called out until he was hoarse for them to stop. Then he watched in horror as all life left Anna's body.

"Why did you let him take Anna?" Zachary said, resentful. "You had to know he would. If he couldn't get the boys, you had to know he'd take Anna."

Bucking up against that resentment, Reg replied, "I didn't want to get involved in the first place. You dragged me into it."

"You could've walked away. Nobody twisted your arm."

Reg looked off. "We were friends. We'd been friends for a long time."

"Friends don't betray each other."

Reg's tone was less defensive now. "I didn't betray you. I tried to help."

"By letting Fritz take Anna?"

As if divulging a deep, dark secret he'd been holding for some time, he told Zachary, "I didn't let Fritz take Anna. She went on her own."

"You're lying."

Reg shook his head back and forth. "She figured out what was going on. She knew Fritz was going to take the boys. She wanted to save her son."

"You're lying," Zachary said again. "You're making this all up to try and justify what you did." Yet the more Reg explained the more it sounded just like something Anna would do.

"She knew you'd try to help her too, and she was convinced it wouldn't work for the plan. She only wanted to save her son, Zachary. But the one couldn't survive without the other. Not early on. And so I had to take both of them. So you see, I didn't betray you. Anna did."

"I still don't understand. Why couldn't you rise above what she wanted to try to save her as well? To try and keep Fritz from taking her."

"Why would I do that?"

"Because you're human?"

"Exactly. And she isn't, and neither is her son. I'm not bound by any law that says I have to help anything that might turn around and—and take my life or the life of someone else."

"She wouldn't do that. She has a soul like you and me. I'm fairly certain she follows the same standards of life you and I do."

"You have no proof of that."

"You have no proof to the contrary. And what does having a soul have to do with saving another, anyway?"

"I have a moral obligation to protect *human* life."

"Your beliefs condone selectively choosing what life you'll save based on your definition of life?"

"Yes. And I happen to believe that a soul sets us apart from all other living things. But then we've had this discussion before haven't we." And indeed they had, and often. He squinted back at Zachary. "If I'm not mistaken, you hold similar values."

"Similar, but clearly different too. But I guess that's just where we'll have to agree to be different. You're comfortable molding situations to fit your ideology. I prefer to mold my ideology to fit the situation. There's too much I don't understand to draw conclusions. A soul, is a soul, is a soul ... even if it appears to be from the deepest, darkest part of space or anywhere else for that matter."

Yet Reg was certain he didn't care to have the discussion presently. "Well in spite of our obvious differences," he continued, "it seems that everyone survived—your son, Anna and her son."

Zachary sat quiet for a moment. Contemplative. And then, "I want to find Anna. I want to find her and free her."

Reg pushed up from the bed and laughed. Headed over to the window to look out. "Have fun, my friend. I'm not signing on for this one."

Zachary got up, returned his wallet with the photo to his pocket and came to stand behind Reg. "It was your carelessness that led Fritz to me, and thanks to you I don't have a home to go back to now. In light of that, I'd say you owe me your cooperation."

Reg turned and looked at Zachary as if to size up the threat. "You're getting bold in your old age," he said. "I like that. And I do feel responsible for what happened today. I'll help you find Anna. Beyond that, I'm through with this. Is that clear?"

"Fair enough," Zachary replied.

Reg turned back to the window. It was dark, and the sky was cloudless. Stars poked holes in the dark canvas as far as he could see. Almost.

"Any clues on where to start looking?"

He glanced back at Zachary, then returned his gaze to the window. "Yeah I've got a clue." He pointed to an area on the horizon where storm clouds had gathered and lightning flashed. Otherwise the sky was clear all around. "See that over there?"

Zachary looked where he pointed. "Yes."

"You have to admit that's an odd sight." Reg moved away from the window, picked up his jacket and slid into it.

Zachary followed him with his eyes. "It's an odd sight. But what are you doing?"

Reg stopped short of leaving and rested his hand on the doorknob. "The best way to locate Anna is to find her son. I learned early on that somehow he was communicating with her. And as you can tell, that's no ordinary storm. That's Jeri. That, my friend, is Anna's son."

* * *

He gave the taxi driver who'd picked him up at the hospital directions but not an address. He didn't speak the directions but offered them via a touch. The very same way he acquired the image to begin with—in the interrogation room. Though the encounter was brief, a quick touch, it gave him enough of a mental picture to direct the taxi driver to this location.

When he matched the picture in his mind with what he saw around him, he instructed the driver to stop. When the fare was asked for, he paid, or rather made the taxi drive think he'd been paid.

Standing on the sidewalk, he looked up, stared at one specific window and moved to make sure he could be seen if anyone happened to stare out from it. He removed the gray scrub shirt he'd been wearing. Extended his arms out, palm-side up, and began. Muscles tense, he began to collect energy from the atmosphere around him. In the sky above him thick, heavy clouds formed. Seconds later, the first streak of lightning hit within yards of where he was.

Chapter 23

Zachary questioned the name shortly after Reg told him. "So that's J-e-r-i?"

Reg eased the car onto the main road that ran in front of the motel. "Mik's idea. I didn't give Anna's son a name. For the seven years he was with me, he pretty much ignored me. And I mean completely ignored me. He depended on Mik for everything." Reg stared ahead as though the memory bothered him but then moved on as though it didn't. "Jeri is actually an acronym. Do you recall that cable you made for Anna? The one she used so she could charge using an electrical outlet? You referred to it as Anna's Electric Recharging Interface. I made a similar one. Hoped that Jeri would eventually use it. I called it a Juvenile Electric Recharging Interface, or JERI adapter. Next thing I knew, Mik was calling Anna's son that."

"I see," Zachary nodded. "But what did you mean when you said you hoped he'd use it?"

"Jeri only knew one way to charge, and that was to draw energy from Mik. He couldn't figure the damn interface out." The frustration of those years and not being able to talk to anyone about it at the time pushed Reg to reveal more. "Mik would accommodate each time Jeri came to him, but for Mik's sake I felt Jeri needed to be more independent. So I tried to help matters along. One

136

particular day, I made it so Mik was preoccupied and conveniently inaccessible to Jeri. I made sure Jeri knew where that charger was, and I waited."

Just as it seemed he was going to make Zachary wait until Zachary prodded, "And what happened?"

Waiting for the stoplight to turn green, Reg pointed forward at the lightning. "That happened. I call it a temper tantrum. And he doesn't have to be outside to have it."

The light changed. Reg drove on. "Imagine walking into a room in your house and seeing that sort of display—*in your house.*"

"That's amazing," Zachary muttered.

"It was damn frightening," Reg countered. "Still is."

* * *

Mik wrestled with his covers, pulled a pillow over his head then launched the pillow across the room. There seemed no reprieve from the constant and intense flashes of lightning. Pushing himself up into a sitting position, he readied himself to go check on the weather. He stepped into a pair of jeans but stopped before putting on a shirt. *That's interesting*, he thought. He'd not taken any pain medication lately, and his shotgun-pellet-riddled chest felt fine. He carefully unwrapped bandages to investigate, and saw by the illumination of the lightning flashes that it looked fine as well.

Not being the first time he'd recovered quickly from an injury that should leave scars but didn't, he accepted the phenomena with little more than a shrug and without another thought. He left the room without donning a shirt and walked down a short hall. Stopping at a window, he stared out.

"What the hell?"

137

There on the sidewalk below, in the precise middle of the lightning storm it seemed, stood his hairless adversary, arms out to his sides, palms up, muscles tense. But what was he doing? Then his head turned, and he stared directly at the window. At Mik.

"Oh that's it," Mik said, provoked by the arrogance or at least what came across as arrogance. "It's on."

Mik pushed so hard, the apartment door slammed shut behind him. He opted to take the stairs over the slow-running elevator, and reached street level much faster. Setting his eyes on his target, he sprinted over and stopped. With mere inches between them Mik growled, "Who are you and what do you want?"

Lightning popped all around. "Touch me," came the reply.

"No way. I'm not making that mistake again." The electric shock he felt when he batted the arm away earlier, in the interrogation room, compelled his response.

And then, just like that, he didn't have to make the mistake because as quick as the lightning that popped all around them, his hands were grabbed, fingers forced between his.

"What the *fuahh*—" The current that ripped through his body took his voice. He couldn't scream. Couldn't think. Couldn't fight. All he could do was stand there and try to break free.

* * *

Ghost squinted at the brightness when he opened his eyes. Was that the front door slamming? And what was up with all the lightning? He found a shirt, pulled it over his head then slid into the jeans to go check. At the window at the end of the hall, he stopped to glance out. His mouth dropped open at the scene on the sidewalk below: Mik and his adversary locked in a submission-style grip.

Apparently it had been the slam of the apartment door that brought Ghost out of his slumber. "Great," Ghost spit out. Now he had to go out there and talk Mik into coming back inside before either one of them were struck by lightning.

He too took the stairs, but stopped short of rushing across the street. Seeing the lightning from the apartment was one thing. Experiencing it was quite another. The charge in the air had the hairs on his arms and the back of his neck standing on end. But back to the more urgent matter, how was he going to get Mik back inside? Perhaps the thicker skin on the palms of his hands and soles of his feet, an attribute of the disease that had rendered him lacking fingerprints, would help protect him if he were struck.

"One can only hope," he muttered upon initiating the only plan he could come up with, charging full speed and barreling into Mik. Seconds before impact lightning struck the pair, or so it seemed. Ghost would later recall that the lightning shot up from the ground though, and not down.

Chapter 24

"Damn," Reg shouted when the sky cleared and the lightning stopped. "We were almost there."

Zachary, eyes still trained ahead, said, "Take that turn up there."

Reg moved past his frustration to follow Zachary's direction. Since he'd been driving, he wasn't able to pay close attention to where they headed. Zachary could. "There," Zachary directed. "Then when you get to that next street, take another right."

* * *

A dazed Ghost pushed himself up to his knees. The lightning had stopped. The storm had cleared. By the glow from a nearby streetlight, he could see Mik on the ground beside him. Ghost shook him, an attempt to rouse him. If Mik could walk on his own then he wouldn't have to lug him. But Mik was out, dead weight and unresponsive no matter how hard he shook his shoulder.

Grabbing an arm, he pulled Mik up. With a supporting arm around his waist, he began the walk to the building entrance, pulling Mik along beside him. He took the elevator this time; he had no desire to drag Mik up the stairs. Once in the apartment, he eased Mik down onto the sofa, then crashed into a nearby chair. He let his head fall back, closed his eyes and then pushed them open again to blankly stare at the ceiling. Why did he feel, all of a sudden, like he needed to go pull the other body into the apartment? He tried a little harder to ignore that feeling but couldn't.

At least he's lighter than Mik, he thought. The internal encouragement did little to wipe the scowl off his face while he lugged the body along and across the street. Nor did it do much to soothe his aching muscles that screamed from doing the activity twice.

Once back inside, he let the body fall into the chair near the sofa. Went back to lock the front door. When he turned to head to his bedroom he stared, stunned. Though one lay prone on the couch, the other half-sitting in a chair, their expressions, their look and even facial features were astonishingly similar. Ghost wrote it off as being tired and headed to his room.

* * *

Reg pulled the car over and both men got out. "Do you feel that?" Reg asked.

"Yes," Zachary acknowledged, allowing himself to be excited. With wide eyes, he examined an arm where the hairs stood up. "But where is he?"

"I don't know," Reg offered while he stood on the street corner and looked under things and inside things: cardboard box remnants, a garbage can lid.

"Are we looking for something specific?"

"A shirt. A coat," Reg said. "Clothing seems to get in the way."

"You mean like this."

Reg turned to find Zachary holding a gray hospital scrub top. "Exactly like that." Reg went over. Took the top and examined it. Saw backward letters and turned it inside out. "Greenfield Mental Hospital?" His mouth gaped open. "Of course. It all makes sense now." Reg looked up to gaze around the empty street once more. "He was here, Zachary. Jeri was here." And then, "Let's get back to the motel. I think I know how we can find him. And then of course find Anna."

* * *

Ghost awoke to the sound of a lamp crashing to the floor. Half-blind from the sunlight streaming in through the hall window, he threw an arm up over his eyes and headed toward the sound of the commotion.

He stopped in the doorway, lowered his arm and squinted. What in the hell was going on? Mik held the lamp cord in one hand. He held a knife in the other. He'd cut the cord from the lamp and was presently stripping at the plastic sheathing to expose the two wires beneath. Because of where Ghost stood, with the sofa blocking the view below Mik's knees, all Ghost could see of Mik when Mik knelt down was his head and shoulders. Ghost walked over and around.

The cord now plugged into the wall, Mik directed the two bared wires toward the unconscious body he straddled.

"No," Ghost yelled at the same time, lunging. An arm locked around Mik's neck, Ghost wrestled him back, pulled hard, careful to avoid the live wires. Not so careful when the plug was pulled from the outlet. "What are you doing? Did getting hit by lightning fry your brain?"

Caught in a headlock, Mik tried to reply. "Let me up. You have to. He's gonna die."

Ghost released a bit, but only a bit of pressure. "He's not gonna die if I don't let you electrocute him."

"Actually," Mik said, "he will. I know it doesn't make sense but you have to believe me."

142

Ghost laughed aloud at that. "Have you forgotten who you're talking to? Why should I believe you? You've already tried to get at him twice today."

"Because he's my brother, Ghost. Sam was right. Besides, look at him. He even looks like me. And if you push him over onto his stomach," the body was currently on its side with his back away from Ghost, "you'll see something else that'll help prove I'm not lying."

So Ghost nudged with his right foot until the body fell onto its stomach. There, at the base of the neck, located lower than Mik's even, was a circular metal disk. Just like Mik's.

"He needs electricity to survive. That's what the disk is for. Please let me help him."

Chapter 25

Reg returned from the motel lobby where he'd gone to use a printer they had there. He also carried the coffee Zachary requested. "We're good to go. I have a few clients who helped me legitimize us as researchers, so we can get into the hospital to see what we can find."

Zachary once again questioned, "But even if he was at Greenfield, he's not there now. Doesn't it make more sense to go back to where we were last night and just wait to see if he shows up again?"

"You want to find Anna," Reg said carefully. "Jeri can lead us to her. If this shirt belonged to him as I suspect it did, then going to Greenfield makes all the sense in the world, even if he's not there now."

Zachary still didn't look convinced. Reg sighed. "You just have to liken it to finding a needle in a haystack. That's a difficult task. Imagine having fifty haystacks, with only one of those containing the needle. Hopefully this trip will help produce enough information to help us identify which haystack to look in. You do want to find Anna in this lifetime, don't you?"

That seemed to do it. "Okay, let's go."

* * *

Ghost sat back on his heels and watched Mik carefully. In fact, he'd been watching for about ten minutes now.

Electric Angel

"See," Mik said after taping the live wires to the metal disk. "It's not hurting him at all. In fact," he said as he eased closed eyelids open, "if you pay attention you'll see his eyes brighten. Almost like they're glowing. The stronger the charge he carries the more they glow."

"What happened to you last night?" Ghost said as if he hadn't heard anything. "What did he do to you?"

"He gave me my memories back: everything I couldn't recall before I came to live with you and Sam. He's had them all this time."

Ghost stared, skeptical. "I see. He gave you your memories back but took your sanity. Because in case you didn't know it, you're talking like a crazy person."

"I know what it must sound like—"

"Good," Ghost said pushing up to stand, "then you'll understand when I call to have him carted away— *Aaaahhh!*" Ghost never made it past where he stood, the stream of current stopping him in his tracks and then, once released from the current's hold, dropping to the floor.

"I wouldn't try that again if I were you."

After a few seconds, Ghost was able to push himself back up onto all fours and then back on his heels. "How'd he do that?" he gasped out. "How the hell did he do that?" Ghost had seen an arm go up just before he got caught up.

"Short answer? He's not human."

Ghost rubbed at the spot on his neck where the current had hit him. "You don't say. But if he's not human, then what is he?"

"He's … sort of an electrical being or entity."

Ghost stared at Mik. "And where does this *being* come from and how does it end up here?"

"I'm not exactly sure where *he* comes from, I just know he's my brother. And he has a name. It's Jeri."

145

Jeri pulled his arms in tight around him as if hugging himself.

"Is he cold?" Ghost asked. "We could get him a blanket."

"No. He's spent his entire life in a mental institution. He was given electric shock treatment on a regular basis. They'd put him in a straitjacket most of the time and I guess it just became a comforting position for him when he charges."

Ghost locked his eyes on Jeri, confused. "Okay. I get that he—that Jeri gave you your memories back, even though I don't really get it, but … what you're recalling now—those would be *his* memories."

"Yes."

"You don't care to explain that."

"No."

* * *

Reg initially handled the file as though it were a sacred scroll, even with the possibility that its contents might not help them find Jeri. Yet he'd gone so long with unanswered questions about what happened to the boys so many years ago, learning anything new might help bring closure.

But his odd handling of the folder brought a curious stare to Zachary's face, and so he worked harder to look less affected. Fortunately, Zachary became as fascinated with the contents, if not for other reasons, so Reg didn't think his original reaction stood out so much.

"There's your proof that he learned how to charge on his own," Zachary spouted. "He got a regular meal every day via electric shock treatment. Amazing."

Reg shook his head in dismay. "I should've known they'd seek help for him. I should've checked local mental facilities sooner." He scrunched his brow then. "But where did they put Mik?"

He went back to the front of the file and saw where a Sam Hawkins had referred Jeri. He recalled from the news story that Mik's last name was now Hawkins. "The referring doctor here must've adopted Mik himself. Which explains why my source couldn't locate him in any of the state-run homes."

Zachary seemed to be intrigued by something completely different though. "Look at that," he said, pointing. "What do you make of that?"

Reg shook his head. "That doesn't make sense. It shows that Jeri is still a patient here, but how can he be?"

"And he was served breakfast this very morning and dinner last night."

Reg closed the file. "Looks like our research is going to take us into the bowels of this hospital. Down where they house the criminally insane."

Chapter 26

Two dead men later, Fritz finally had the file taken from Reg's house in his possession. He couldn't help but wonder if he'd find anything else of value, other than Zachary's current address that now stood to do him no good whatsoever.

The numbskull thieves hadn't even been careful enough to throw Reg off track by making it tougher for him to figure out just what had been taken. This, of course, lessened the chances of catching Zachary at all. Even so, this didn't bother him. He'd only planned on using Zachary to get to Reg, who most certainly knew where the boys were or at least knew how to find them.

But what else was in the file, he wondered. It certainly held a lot of paper, including—"A diary?" Eager, he opened up to the first page, flipped to the second and then the third. It seemed to mention each day with the boys, if not but a few sentences, starting with the day Reg took them and ending with the day they disappeared.

* * *

Impossible.

Ghost stared at Mik's chest. The bandages were gone, as were the wounds. Mik caught him looking. "Jeri took care of that," he said before Ghost could ask. "And don't ask me how because I don't even know myself."

148

"Good to know I'm not the only one in the dark. But since you do seem to know *some* things about him, maybe you can explain why he has no body hair to speak of. No eyebrows, no eyelashes. That's just weird."

"I don't know exactly but it probably has to do with the amount of electrical current he has to maintain to survive. Somehow it affects hair growth."

Jeri moved to sit up. Pulled the taped wires loose. Mik immediately disconnected the cord from the outlet. Jeri's eyes were quite bright to Ghost, and did seem to glow.

"I don't appreciate the way you zapped me a minute ago," Ghost said. "I think you owe me an apology."

A hand went out and Ghost reached to shake it. Current ripped through his body once again. Reacting instinctively Mik grabbed hold of Ghost in an attempt to free him only to find himself in the same position. Both fell back when Jeri turned loose first.

Both lay there moaning for quite a few seconds until Ghost found his voice. "Good to know you have such control over him."

Jeri extended a hand out to Mik. "No," Mik said at the offer of assistance. "It's okay. I can get up on my own." And he did.

Ghost took a little longer getting to his feet, but then he'd just recently been hit. "How did you survive seven years with him?"

Mik shook his head. "It's not his fault. He's been isolated in that damn mental institution for so long, he's forgotten how to operate around others."

"Mental institution? You know they don't usually isolate people at a mental hospital unless there's a big problem. Actually, that's usually the reason for institutionalizing them in the first place. You're not just a little concerned about that?"

"There's nothing wrong with him."

"Right. I meet guys like that every day. Mik, you said it yourself. He's not human. Maybe the mental institution is the best place for him."

Mik whipped his head around. "I'm not taking him back there. There's nothing wrong with him. Not anything they can fix anyway. I guess the question is whether you're on board with my helping him. Can I trust you?"

"Really." Ghost chortled. "You're really going to ask me that. C'mon, you know me." He offered a fist up. Mik bumped it with his. "I've always got your back, right?"

Jeri had, closely watched the exchange and offered a fist up. Ghost stared at the fist directed at him and turned to Mik. "Yeah, I got your back but I'm not 'bumping' that. No way. He's all yours."

* * *

After introductions, Reg and Zachary followed Monty into the elevator. "We're particularly interested in meeting Jeri," Reg said.

A low laugh erupted from within the nurse's bulky dark frame. "You mean 'bright eyes.' That's what I call him most of the time. Sometimes his eyes are so bright it seems like they glow."

Reg and Zachary shared a confused look. How could Jeri be in two places at once? Monty misinterpreted their shared look as meaning they didn't believe his comment. "You'll see," he said. "He's right over here."

Monty stepped out of the elevator. Headed over to one of five doors that lined the far side of the hall. "Bright eyes," he said, rapped on the outside of one door. "You have company." He looked toward Reg and Zachary as they approached. "He don't talk much though. In fact, I don't recall him ever saying one word."

The barred observation window on the door was small. Reg peered in first. "See what I mean?" Monty roared laughter. "Brightest eyes you've ever seen, right?"

"Yeah," Reg said before he stepped away for Zachary to look.

"Bet you thought I was telling you a fib," Monty continued. Reg and Zachary shared another look, but they waited until they were outside to discuss what it meant.

Walking down the sidewalk toward the parking lot, Zachary said, "Do you think he knows the cell is empty?"

"I don't think it's empty to him. Think about it, Zachary. It's a perfect cover-up. And it means Jeri planned this. If Monty believes he's there, then he won't report that he's actually not there. No one will be looking for him, and he can proceed with whatever plans he has."

"Plans?" Zachary's tone was questioning, in a worried way. "You make it sound like he's up to something."

Reg opened the driver's-side door. "You forget I lived with him for seven years," he said, getting in.

"Yes," Zachary said. Settled into the passenger's seat. "Until he was seven. Not nearly long enough to surmise that he had an agenda worthy of being scrutinized now."

"You saw that file. You know what landed him here."

"No one knew how to deal with him." Zachary had seen the file, and that was what he'd read. Why would Reg infer otherwise?

Reg put the key in the ignition and started the car. "Yes, but ultimately he ended up here because he killed two police officers."

"The file said the judge acquitted him and Mik."

"The judge in the case didn't see what I saw. Nor did he have the knife Jeri used to cut the cord to that drink machine. The cord he used to charge with, so when he and Mik joined hands they'd create enough electricity to do those two officers in."

Still parked and with the car running, Reg decided to finish making his point. "I'll help you find Jeri so you can find Anna. After that, I don't want anything more to do with any of this."

"Fair enough," Zachary answered. "But since he's not here, where do you suggest we look now?"

"I guess we go back with your idea. We'll just park around where we found the shirt. Jeri's bound to be around there somewhere. And since the little lightning storm he created last night ended so abruptly, I suspect he's with Mik now too. He uses him to discharge all that pent-up current."

* * *

Fritz studied the folder taken from Reg's house throughout the day. Told his secretary to hold any and all calls. He pored through the diary and back through it again. He called Bill on one occasion, and just now had caught sight of something written in pen on the inside cover as he went to close it.

"Sam Hawkins," he read aloud. Perhaps related to the officer Mik Hawkins. Perhaps Sam Hawkins had knowledge of where this Mik Hawkins lived. "The police won't give me his address," he continued to think aloud. "Perhaps you will."

Chapter 27

The three sat around a small kitchen table. Jeri now wore one of Mik's shirts, since Mik couldn't locate the one Jeri came out of the night before. And he'd looked all around the area where he'd been standing. As they sat around and finished off a box of Pop-Tarts, Mik commented that someone must've taken it.

Jeri ate around the sides of one Pop-Tart. Watched Mik devour his and did the same. "Juice," he said afterward.

"So it can talk," Ghost said. Jeri reached over with a hand and rewarded Ghost's sarcasm by shocking him.

"Stop that," Ghost shot back, moved his chair over.

"More juice," Jeri repeated.

"How could he want more juice?" Ghost said, irritated. "He drank the whole carton. By the way," he said to Mik, "that's coming out of your paycheck."

"I don't think he means orange juice."

"But I thought you took care of that with the lamp cord."

"Apparently he needs more."

Both Mik and Ghost watched as Jeri, his eyes showing only the faintest glimmering, slowly leaned forward until his head came to rest on the table.

"Help me get him back over to the outlet," Mik said. Ghost groaned, but complied.

Mik plugged the cut lamp cord back in, taped the bared wires back in place. Yet things didn't seem to be moving along as they did before. "I don't know," Mik said, growing frustrated. "Maybe he needs a more powerful source."

A wicked grin played on Ghost's lips. "You don't say." He got up and headed for his bedroom. With no fingerprints, Ghost couldn't pass a background check. Therefore he couldn't carry firearms. But he could carry Tasers and stun guns. He walked back into the room ready for action. "I'm going to enjoy this," he said, aimed and fired the Taser from the door. Both probes implanted themselves in Jeri's upper left shoulder. He then eagerly moved over to press the stun gun against Jeri's upper arm. He repeatedly used both devices until the batteries ran down.

Jeri raised up at once. Pulled the two probes from his shoulder.

"Better?" Mik asked.

"Yes," Jeri replied as they all moved to stand.

Jeri extended his right arm toward Ghost as if to offer him his thanks with a handshake. "No way am I falling for that," Ghost said. "Forget about it."

So Jeri raised a palm and pushed out. Ghost literally flew backward then flipped over the sofa, rolling and then landing on the floor.

A cell phone rang. Seconds later Mik moved to tower over Ghost. "The hospital just called. Somebody visited Sam about twenty minutes ago. Right after they left, Sam took a turn for the worse. They suspect the guy did something to Sam but they don't know what. They think we should come right away. Sam's not doing good."

Ghost grabbed at the coffee table in front of the sofa. Moved as though he'd been drinking all morning. Then finally managed to pull it together. "Why the hell would anyone want to do anything to Sam?"

"I don't know. Maybe we can get some information out of him to help us figure that out."

Ghost turned to look at Jeri. "We're leaving him here, right?"

"Why would we do that?"

"Is it really safe to take him along?"

"He'll be fine."

"Who said I was referring to *his* safety?"

At the car, parallel parked in front of their apartment complex, Ghost slid into the driver's seat, inserted the key and groaned at the nonproductive winding whir of the engine attempting but failing to turn over. "Great. Looks like we're going to need a jump."

Jeri leaned over the back of the front seat. Ghost immediately jumped from the car. A finger went to the key and the car started.

Ghost waited until Jeri settled back before returning to his spot behind the wheel and drove on to the hospital.

* * *

Any hope of questioning Sam disappeared when they heard the sound of the ventilator that was helping him breathe. "I'll leave you two alone with him," the nurse said.

Ghost shook his head. "I just don't get it. The guy had to have done something to him. He was fine when we left him yesterday. Ornery but fine."

"Yeah," Mik agreed. "Let's go see if anyone saw anything that might help us figure out what happened."

Jeri stood in the hall outside. Mik spoke to him as they passed. "Just stay right there. We'll be back in a second."

155

When asked, they were directed to Sandra, the same nurse who'd been in the room with Sam the day before.

"I'm sorry," she said. "All I can tell you is that the man said he was a relative. And I only left the room for a second when I had to race back because the alarm on Sam's oxygen machine went off. It had been unplugged, but Sam shouldn't have been as bad off as he was. It just doesn't make sense."

"So it was just the one guy," Ghost said.

"Yes. He was about your height. Had a Mediterranean look about him." She stopped talking to look past them. "Was he with you?" she asked, glancing over to where Jeri had been standing. Before they could answer, a shrill beep sounded.

"The ventilator," the nurse said, her eyes wide.

All three raced across the hall and into the room. The nurse went to the ventilator and then sighed relief. "It's all right. It just went off because Sam is breathing on his own now." She glanced over at Jeri. "You should come around more often. You seem to bring good luck."

"Juice," Jeri said, those odd colorless eyes rolling back in his head. Mik and Ghost both rushed over and caught him before his knees gave out.

Sandra took a step toward them but stopped, looking uncertain. "Is he all right?"

"Oh he's fine," Mik replied as he and Ghost walked with him to the door. "We'll come back tomorrow and check on Sam. Call us before then if you think he can talk."

Out in the hall and jostling Jeri along, Mik hissed to Ghost, "What do you mean you didn't bring your Taser and stun gun?"

"The batteries were dead, remember."

156

The elevator doors at the end of the hall opened; they moved hurriedly to take advantage. Ghost managed to get a hand in a pocket to flash a badge to someone who looked like they might want to ride down with them, and the door closed.

"What now?" Ghost asked.

"I don't know"

"Well you better think of something soon or we're going to have to call someone to jumpstart the car."

"That's it," Mik said. "We'll jumpstart him." The elevator doors slid open.

Chapter 28

Reg intended to park where they'd parked the night before. Problem was, another car had parked there and two men sat inside. He drove on.

"Let's make the block," he told Zachary, "and park farther back."

"You think it's just a coincidence that someone else is parked there?" Zachary asked. The street didn't appear to be all that busy. Most cars seemed to come and go. Especially now that the lunch hour approached.

"Probably," Reg said, but took a moment to come up with that single word.

They sat for ten minutes according to Reg's watch, before a car pulled up in front of an apartment building across the way. "Still think it's a coincidence."

The other two men visibly straightened in their vehicle as well.

Three doors opened on the car that had pulled up and parked and three men got out.

"My God," Reg voiced disbelief. "It's both of them."

Zachary simply stared in stunned silence. "I don't know who the third guy is though."

The three went inside. A few seconds later, the two men in the parked car in front of Reg and Zachary got out. They brashly tucked pistols into the waistlines of their pants and headed toward the building as well. The second they stepped inside and the door closed behind them, Zachary threw his door open and got out. Reg immediately got out and followed after him. Pulled him aside once he caught up with him. "Are you insane? They have guns."

"I can't just sit out here and do nothing. Not when I can actually do something this time."

"I don't think getting yourself killed qualifies as doing something." Reg looked around. "Come on. I've got another idea."

* * *

Mik's idea—to find and use a defibrillator—worked well enough, but next time Jeri lost his charge, they had to be ready. On the way back, they stopped at a store to pick up fresh batteries. Ghost quickly replaced the depleted ones and holstered both devices.

"There," he said to Mik. "Happy now?"

Before Mik could respond, the apartment's front door flew open. Two men with pistols drawn stepped inside. "Come with us and nobody gets hurt."

"That's what you think," Mik said. "Jeri?" A stream of current hit both men. They fell to the floor, but Ghost, Mik and Jeri weren't around to see it. They were already running down the stairs.

"Aw man," Ghost said, seeing his car. All four tires were flat.

A car pulled up beside theirs. The driver stepped out, looked over the top of the car. "Get in," he said. When they didn't move, he added, "It's me—Reg."

With no clear indication that any of them recognized Reg or knew who he was, Reg wasn't holding a gun on them, which meant he was a better bet just then than the men upstairs, who might already be racing down the stairs after them. All three got into the car. Quite a few blocks away and when he was certain no one had followed, Reg pulled over, put the car in park and turned in his seat. "My God, I never thought I'd see you two again."

Finally a glimmer of recognition. "I don't recall you really seeming to care," Mik said.

"Perhaps not as much as I should have, but then I'm not your father." He nodded toward Zachary. "He is."

"You both resemble your mother so much." Zachary's voice was so thick with emotion, he choked the words out. "Please help me find her."

"Do either one of you know something about why those goons were at our apartment?" Ghost said. "Seems kind of odd how you showed up just in time."

"They were sent by the same guy who's been trying to find Mik and Jeri," Reg said. "Doesn't seem like he's ever going to give up."

The information didn't seem to affect Mik at all, and Jeri continued to look disinterested as usual.

"He's holding your mother captive," Zachary added. "Reg thinks Jeri can help us find her." Still Mik didn't seem impressed. "Not to mention that Jeri's dying, and she can teach him what he needs to know to survive."

Mik all but laughed at that. "Oh, you're really reaching for it now."

"Am I?" Zachary said. "He can't hold a charge. That shouldn't be the case. He has to be able to take in energy and store it. Anna— His mother can help him figure out how to do this. If he doesn't figure it out soon, he'll die."

Chapter 29

Fritz hadn't gotten any information out of Sam, yet he was able to glean an address from an unguarded folder laying out at the nurses station, and managed to scribble down the address before he was caught looking. He'd called his men directly after he left the hospital to give them the details, and now listened carefully as they told him what happened.

"You were knocked back by a surge of electrical current," Fritz repeated after having the call transferred to the phone on his desk. "Fascinating. And you say there were three men in the apartment instead of just the one. What did you find when you searched the apartment? ... I see," he said when told about the lamp cord with the wires stripped back. "Well, stay close to your phones. I'll need you to attend a funeral. Perhaps tomorrow or the day after that. I'll let you know more as soon as I know more."

Fritz then ended that call and initiated another. "Bill," he said. "I need you to get the portable containment unit ready for use."

* * *

Mik and Ghost walked with Jeri between them, supported him on either side as they helped him up the flight of stairs to Room 247.

161

"I don't get it," Mik said after they'd eased Jeri down. "Ghost zapped him all the way over here with that damn stun gun."

"He needs you." Reg walked in from outside, and produced what appeared to be a cable from a deeper pocket in the front of his trousers. He tossed it over to Mik. "Remember that?"

Mik caught the cable and stared as though seeing an old friend for the first time in far too long. "Yes, I do."

"Then you know what to do with it."

Mik secured one of the magnetic disks to the metal disk at the back of his neck, then sat on the edge of the bed where Jeri lay. He turned Jeri's head slightly and secured the other magnetic end to the circular disk implanted at the base of his neck.

He might have recalled the cable and what it was used for but it became clear right away that he didn't exactly recall how to proceed. Muscles contracted and retracted. His back arched and at one point he cried out. Ghost bolted forward in response, ignored Reg's warning that started with, "I wouldn't," and ended with, "do that," as Ghost flew backward past him due to the amount of current that hit him when he grabbed hold of Mik. Ghost slowly stood, rubbing his head where he'd hit the wall.

"It's not hurting him," Reg told Ghost. "Mik just has to get used to the process again." Shortly after he said that Mik did grow quiet and even moved to lay on his side, his back to Jeri's back.

"What are they doing?" Ghost asked once he found his voice.

Yet it was Zachary who answered, understanding but disbelieving. "They're creating electricity."

Reg nodded. "Exactly. Not surprised you picked up on that."

"That must've been what they were doing the day they were born," Zachary continued.

"It's exactly what they were doing," Reg confirmed. "And it seems abundantly clear now that the type of electricity they generate is the only kind that will sustain Jeri for any length of time. Honestly, I'm not sure how he's made it this long without Mik's help."

"All we can do is speculate," Zachary said. "Perhaps that's why he left Greenfield—because he knew he needed what only Mik could offer." Zachary sighed then. "As hard as it is for me to say because of the way things played out, it's a good thing Fritz didn't find what he was looking for that night. More important, it's a good thing he doesn't have any real knowledge of what they're capable of. There'd be no stopping him."

Reg's look turned dismal as he rubbed at the back of his neck. "Bad news. The folder his men took from my house had a diary in it. One I'd been keeping every day since I had the boys until I lost track of them. I'm pretty sure he knows everything about the boys now."

* * *

A lot of what Mik couldn't remember about his past returned when he met Jeri in the street in front of the apartment the night of the lightning storm, which he now understood Jeri had caused. At twenty-four however, he pushed to understand the logic of a not-so-mature seven-year-old taking his memories to give them back to him later.

As he lay with his back to his brother, a cable connecting them, he shared his frustration via nonverbal thoughts packed with emotion. "You shouldn't have done that," he scolded. "I wouldn't have done that to you."

A feeling was returned. Raw emotion. Jeri was sorry, very sorry. And Mik found he couldn't be angry at him beyond the initial frustration. "It's all right. I know you don't understand a lot of things."

Jeri's positive response to that eased Mik's mind. Jeri hadn't understood. Understanding was beyond him.

* * *

"How much longer will they be like that?" Ghost asked after an hour passed and Mik still lay silent, staring ahead.

"I suspect Jeri needed a pretty good charge," Reg offered. "But it shouldn't be much longer now." And indeed, Mik stirred and then sat up. He pulled the magnetic disk from where it was attached on his neck, then detached the one from Jeri's neck and stuffed the cable in a pocket.

Jeri sat up as well, and turned to reveal eyes that glowed.

"Bright eyes," Zachary said. "That must've been what Monty was talking about."

"Monty," Jeri repeated. "Bright eyes."

"Is it just me, or is he starting to sound a lot like Dustin Hoffman in *Rain Man*?" Ghost commented.

"Who's Monty?" Mik said.

Reg told him about the trip they made to Greenfield. "Monty thinks Jeri's still in his cell. He apparently takes him his food and meds and returns with an empty tray. I don't mind telling you, but that's a little frightening to me."

Mik squinted, not the first time he'd looked at Reg as though he questioned his thinking. "So he didn't want to be found out. It's not like he killed anybod—" He stopped short. Seemingly disturbed by Reg's very readable expression. He then continued, yet on a slightly different line of conversation. "Wait a minute. Why would your first instinct be one of fright? I could understand if you were talking about a stranger: someone you didn't know. But that's not the case here."

Reg wasted no time sharing what sparked his fear and the look of dread on his face. "Did he kill those two officers that night?"

Mik glanced at Jeri. "Why don't you ask him? He's standing right there."

"Because he won't talk to me. He's never talked to me."

"That's because he knows it wouldn't matter. Experience has proven that you're going to believe what you want to believe."

"I saw what happened that night. I was parked on the street and standing just outside my car."

"I was standing right next to him—"

"Okay," Zachary butted in. "This isn't getting us anywhere. Reg, you said you'd help me find Anna, and after that you were done. So let's just stick with that plan. Mik," he said, "does Jeri know where we can find Anna? I know she can help him, and I desperately want to help free her."

"He knows how to find her," Mik said. "He took me with him to visit her on several occasions. Though not in a conventional way."

Zachary's eyes brightened with hope. "How then? How can we find her?"

"Your best chance is to take him back to Greenfield and let him lead you via the power lines he's been traveling all these years."

When he and Reg had visited Jeri's now-empty cell, Zachary recalled the wires hanging down from behind the cot-like bed. Mik looked around the room before adding, "He could probably lead you from here, but it'd be a

165

different route. He'd have to have time to find her. Especially since he isn't able to maintain a consistent level of energy."

Zachary responded to Mik's drop in enthusiasm, his obvious concern for Jeri's welfare. "Anna can help him with that," he encouraged. "She'd do anything for him." He closed his eyes against sudden moisture in them. "Anything. I can vouch for that."

Chapter 30

They decided to check out of the motel at the odd time of three-thirty in the afternoon. Reg and Zachary, the last two out of the room, walked together. "I'm not the bad guy here," Reg told Zachary.

"Nobody said you were."

"Yeah, but you're all thinking it. You know, it's just as bad to judge someone because of how they feel about something."

Their room had been on the second floor. Zachary stopped walking at the bottom of the stairs that led down. Far enough away from the car so that no one would hear, he said, "If you'd like, you can drop us off at a car rental place. We can rent something so you can be on your way. You held up your end of the bargain. You said you'd stay long enough to help me find Anna. It's clear that helping Jeri bothers you. I wouldn't want to put you out."

Reg nodded and bit his lip. "Technically, you haven't found Anna yet. So I haven't held up my end of the bargain. I made a promise and I intend to keep it."

Zachary nodded back. "Then we should be on our way."

* * *

Mik leaned against the car next to where Jeri sat perched on the back of the trunk. Spoke to Ghost, who'd taken a position in front of him. "You don't have to go along with us, you know? This could get pretty weird."

"I'm into weird."

"Yeah. Well, it could get a lot weirder. Maybe even dangerous."

Ghost shrugged. "I'm into dangerous. Besides, he's your brother, right? Makes him my brother too."

Mik turned to Jeri as though he'd said something, though no sound had been made. "Jeri wants me to tell you something."

"Yeah. What?"

"You know when he zapped you earlier today and sent you flying backwards over the couch."

Ghost answered, a little more guarded this time, "Yeah. I remember."

"Jeri said to tell you to look at your fingertips."

As if something were wrong with his hearing, Ghost responded with, "What?"

"Your fingertips, look at them."

Ghost opened both hands and gawked. "My God," he stammered. "Oh my God." Hands held in front of him like a surgeon getting ready to operate, he ran to a side window, breathed on it and then pressed a finger where condensation from his breath had formed. "Ha! Look at that."

Mik now stood next to Ghost. "Jeri said you're welcome."

"Do you know what this means?" Ghost said. "I can pass a background check now. I can get a gun. A real gun." He'd been trying for over six months, but because he lacked fingerprints had to submit tons of paperwork that never seemed to make it through.

"And somehow," Mik said of this revelation, "hearing this doesn't make me feel any safer."

168

* * *

Fritz scoured the online obituaries a second time. The injection of potassium chloride wasn't immediately lethal, but Sam should've been dead by now. And of course for his plan to work he had to be dead.

He went back to the beginning and searched once more. Perhaps he'd died and they just hadn't posted it yet. Anxious to know, he decided to call the hospital.

* * *

Reg took the Greenfield exit. Moved toward the four-way stop and into the left lane to follow the signs. "No," Mik said at once. "Jeri said go right."

And so it continued, with Mik speaking for Jeri to prevent anything getting lost in translation. Jeri had so little experience speaking, recalling words, or even knowing which one to use, it just made more sense for Mik to speak for him. It was when the directions took them back into Newark and into the projects, going in circles it seemed, that Mik spoke up. "Pull into that alley," he pointed. "Jeri's traveling old paths. He needs a fresh signal, or else we could be riding around in circles for a while."

With the car idling, Jeri and Mik got out and walked deeper into the alley. They didn't have to go far before they found the empty metal housing where an electrical meter had been with words scribbled on cardboard that read: "Hot!!!" and beneath that "Live wire!"

Jeri went right to work. Mik gave a thumbs-up to those waiting in the car.

"Good," Reg muttered. "I'm fairly certain this isn't a safe place to be even in the daytime." With shadows growing longer by the second, getting out of the projects soon made a lot more sense than sitting around in an alley.

Ghost stared out the back window and around. "You know, it sort of makes sense now why Mik always ended up here." Zachary's expression, when he turned in his seat, begged for clarification. "Well not exactly here, just this part of town. When we were younger and even after that, Mik would often just vanish. Even a few nights ago, when he was shot, this is where they found him. He never recalled why or how he ended up where he did."

"That's interesting," Reg said. "Does make one wonder," Zachary added.

A series of small explosions drew their attention to the alley before them as three working electrical meters blew up. White smoke billowed out and filled the air. Seconds later, Mik and Jeri appeared out of the smoke, rushing toward the car.

"Let's go," Mik said, piling in after Jeri and pulling the back door shut behind him, "before someone comes out to investigate."

Chapter 31

Anna raced across power lines, high-voltage and low-voltage, to meet him, to find him, to direct him. Days without a signal left her anxious and worried. Had she asked too much of him too soon? Yet he grew weaker every day. If he didn't find her soon he might not be able to find her at all, and she wouldn't be able to help him.

She surged along, the signal getting stronger. Surged along until she found him.

* * *

No more driving in circles. Jeri seemed to know exactly the way they needed to go. Mik continued to speak for him though the directions didn't come quite as frequently. The road they were on now led away from the projects, into a more industrialized section of the city.

"We're close now," Mik said after a long moment with no directions at all. And then they saw it. A substation surrounded by chain-link fence. Signs secured to the fence at spaced intervals that read: "No trespassing. Property of Anderson Electric."

Reg pulled off the road close to the gated entrance and the dirt road that led to it.

"Well, it's locked," Reg offered, noting a weather-protected keypad mounted off to the side as Mik pushed his door open to exit the car, Jeri nudging him along and even pushing.

"I'm getting out," Mik barked, but then blew off being aggravated to follow Jeri, now headed toward the gate.

Ghost followed him, Zachary behind them. Reg then shut off the car and headed over as well. "Anybody ever heard of a plan?" he grumbled, his words coming just as Jeri, his right hand on the keypad, found the code needed to enter.

"Amazing," Zachary sighed, recalling the keypad just outside the cell door when they'd visited Jeri's cell. "That must be how he escaped at Greenfield."

The group continued toward the station house. Reg continued to point out problems they might encounter if they didn't slow down and think. "Fritz isn't an idiot," he huffed as he rushed to catch up. "He's already killed more than a few men trying to get what he wants. You've got to believe that he keeps his fingers on the pulse of what goes on here. For God's sake, would somebody listen to me?"

Mik reached forward to stop Jeri. Held him by an arm as he turned to address Reg. "Okay," Mik said, "what? Do you know something specifically that we need to know about?"

"I'm a little concerned," Reg said. "Concerned about how much Fritz knows."

Mik's brow furrowed. "Fritz?"

"Yes. The man who's been after you and Jeri all these years."

"The man who took Anna," Zachary added, not doing a good job of hiding his bitterness.

Reg nodded. "And yes, the man who took Anna."

Jeri pulled free from Mik's hold. "Doesn't look like he's worried about Fritz," Mik said, and took up following after

Jeri once more, as did Ghost and Zachary, who dismissed Reg's concerns as easily as the others had—in spite of knowing more. In spite of understanding the dangers Reg stated concern about.

Jeri pushed the unlocked door open and headed toward another door, to another keypad.

"I'm telling you," Reg said as he stared around. "Things shouldn't be this easy. I don't have a good feeling about this."

"Doesn't sound like you have a good feeling about anything," Ghost remarked.

Jeri repeated the procedure of placing a hand on the code pad and seeming to concentrate. Then he keyed a code and pushed the just-unlocked door open. In the middle of this room sat another room of sorts, with its own ceiling and walls. For cracking the code on this keypad, Jeri used a different procedure. He simply aimed and sent a charge from his right palm. A voice that Zachary identified at once filled the air around them. "Anna," he gasped, ran toward the observation window and peered in.

"It's a trap, Zachary. Leave now. Before it's too late."

"I'm not leaving here without you. How do we get you out of here?"

"I'm sorry," came another voice. Fritz's voice. "There'll be no getting out for any of you."

The door they'd entered through slammed shut. Another door slid closed over that one. A solid thud defined its thickness.

"Of course I considered how to contain Anna should she happen to escape the containment chamber, so don't look for her *offspring* to be able to help you find a way out. And so, without further ado," his voice trailed off as though he'd turned his head away, and all anyone heard was the name

Bill and what sounded like instructions. He then spoke directly once more. "This will only take a minute."

All heads turned toward a new sound in the room. The canister-shaped device was about the size of a scuba diver's air tank, but with switches and lights not on any scuba gear, and sat off in a corner. Zachary immediately shared his stunned disbelief, "My God. That's what they used to take Anna. He's going to do it again. He's going to take Jeri."

Then Jeri began to react the same way Anna had: emitted an unnatural ear-piercing scream as muscles locked and the inevitable began to happen. Seconds into the process, he reached out toward Mik as though asking for help, the identical way Anna did when Zachary couldn't move at all because he was tied to a chair.

Mik could move, and did. Fought the current to try to make a connection, yet couldn't get close. He continued to try until he could no longer stand. He fell at the same time Jeri did, collapsed onto all fours. Jeri's form fell in a lifeless heap onto the concrete floor.

"Thank you all for being so cooperative," Fritz said. "I'll be sending Bill in now. Do keep in mind that I have a gun and, forgive the cliché, I'm not afraid to use it."

The solid door slid open. The other door was pushed open by Bill. He walked over, retrieved the canister and carried it out. Both doors shut once again, sealing them all inside.

All of them, except Jeri.

Chapter 32

Zachary felt helpless that night so many years ago but he realized, after watching Mik try to help Jeri, there was nothing he could've done to prevent Anna from being taken. Mik had tried, though it didn't seem to help him deal with what had just happened either. "Jeri," he muttered, shook at the body and then again when he got no response, "Jeri."

Reg took the few steps over. Reached out with a comforting hand that Mik instantly slapped away when he spotted it in his peripheral vision.

There had been a steady glow inside the containment room. No one realized how much the glow influenced the lighting all around until the glow became dimmer and the brightness all around lessened.

"I've lost my son," Anna said. "I've lost him."

The mourning silence that followed ended with a different voice being broadcast over the speakers. "Put the gun down."

"Sam?" Ghost said.

"You're alive?" Fritz's voice replied. "Impossible. I injected you with a lethal dose of potassium chloride."

Mik gently eased Jeri's form down and stood. "That Fritz guy must've been the one who visited Sam earlier today. But how is he here now?"

"You have my boys. Where are they?"

To Sam's question, Fritz said, "I'm sorry. I don't know who you're talking about. And since I have no use for you—" A shot rang out and then another. After that, both doors that stood between them and the exit opened and Bill stepped in. "You're free to go now," he said, visibly shaken.

Fritz lay on the floor in a puddle of blood, the shot Sam fired a direct hit. But Fritz had fired first.

Once at his side, Ghost pulled at Sam's bloodstained shirt. Sam weakly grabbed his wrist. "Did I kill the son of a bitch?"

Ghost heard Mik's cry at seeing Sam, but his heart was too full to speak at first. In his day, no one could outshoot Sam Hawkins. When they were children, he often took Mik and Ghost hunting or to the shooting range. "You nailed it Sam," he at last was able to say. "Bull's-eye."

Sam turned his head to look up at Mik. "Sorry I didn't tell you about your brother sooner. He was a good kid. I just didn't understand about him when I first met him. I didn't know. I'm sorry."

Mik held it together for the moment. For Sam.

"He's the reason I'm here, you know," Sam said. "He fixed everything. Hell, I can even breathe on my own. You have any idea how good that feels after all these years? Anyway, he led me here. Said you and Ghost were in trouble. Explained to me how to get here. When you see him again, you tell him I appreciate what he did for me. You tell him that, okay?"

After that Sam grew silent.

Too silent.

"He's gone," Ghost said through a sob.

Just behind them, the canister began to visibly arc electricity, and Anna called out for them to bring it to her. Bill moved forward to follow through, an indication that his allegiance to Fritz had been forced and not voluntary. Grabbed hold and reacted at once to the electrical current that held him in place. Ghost ran forward, grabbed hold of Bill and pulled him loose.

To those who stared, stunned at his not being affected, Ghost said, "Extra-thick palms. Good insulation." That part of his disease, Jeri hadn't taken care of.

"If you could just bring it into the room, that will be far enough," Anna said.

Even with thicker-than normal palms, Ghost struggled to stay focused. Before he picked the canister up, he mapped out his route. None the worse for the surge of voltage, he set it down just inside the door.

"Now what, Anna?" Zachary said. "What do we do now?"

"Release him. Then release me into the room."

All eyes turned to Bill. "I can release Anna into the room, but I don't know how to operate the canister. Fritz never showed me."

Zachary turned to look at the canister, his eyes glassing over at some memory. "I watched the one man operate the unit years ago. I can just reverse the process from the switches here."

Reg stepped in then, to point out the obvious. "You'd be electrocuted the instant the entity is released."

"You mean Jeri," Mik corrected. "And he won't be electrocuted because he's not going to be here. Show me the switches. Jeri will protect me. The same way he's always protected me."

Zachary nodded. "Of course." And then he showed him.

177

With no observation window for the main room, they couldn't see things as they happened. Yet they'd put the speaker on two-way so they could communicate. At some point Mik would direct Bill by letting him know when to release Anna back out into the substation yard, where she would then take Jeri and leave, drawing from the raw power the substation offered to break the hold that held her captive for over twenty years.

After a few tense moments Mik spoke. "Let her out. And let us out too."

He'd said "us," and those watching breathed a collective sigh of relief.

Mik walked out first, and then the reanimated Jeri. His eyes blazed light, and Mik instructed everyone not to touch him. Instead they followed him out into the substation yard where, with his help, Anna would free herself and take him with her. But he stopped short of going into the yard itself.

"What's he doing?" Ghost asked Mik.

"I'm not sure." They'd all stopped a few feet away.

Jeri, his right arm out, directed a stream of current that forked and stirred up two separate dust devil-like clouds of dirt. They started small and grew to about six feet in height before dissipating. Then Jeri started again. The second time, the dust devils lasted longer before disappearing. Upon his third try, Jeri extended a tense left arm out, fingers spread, and Mik reacted.

"He can't recall exactly," he muttered as he headed over, understanding in his tone. Once next to his brother, he placed the fingers of his right hand in the open spaces between Jeri's fingers, who subsequently clamped down. At once, the dust devils thickened in form and substance and this time when they dissipated, two human forms were

178

revealed. The two men lay on the ground fully dressed in their uniforms.

"My God," Reg breathed out. "It's the two officers who died that night." He then recalled what Mik had said before he headed over. "Jeri must've needed Mik to help him remember what they looked like."

Yet the two forms were just that—two lifeless forms. Jeri left Mik's side and headed over to kneel between the officers. He extended both arms and stayed that way until a blinding ball of light formed in each palm. He then turned each palm and pushed down. Both men coughed and spit out water as they pushed up to stand. Instead of confusion however, they simply seemed satisfied just to be back in their own bodies.

Ghost stepped forward to address Jeri. "Can you do that for Sam? You helped him once."

"I can't," Jeri said, sounding and looking dismal. "I'm sorry."

He headed off then. Toward the substation yard, and home. Ghost turned to Mik. "I don't understand. Why can't he?"

"He can't bring a soul back once its reached its destination. But he can usually pull them in and hold them before they get too far away. Like he did with the two officers."

Ghost held all other questions for the moment. Already clouds had gathered, with thick, heavy billows over the spot where Jeri stood. The air became thick with current. Lightning flashed, and the current increased. Electricity arced across high-voltage lines and all around him. Those standing nearby moved back farther. Ran for the station house for protection. After the grandest of finales, including lightning so intense they had to cover their eyes

179

to avoid being temporarily blinded, they headed back out. Everything was surreally the same. And then Mik, pulling up the rear, collapsed. A quick evaluation revealed no pulse.

"No," Zachary whispered, pulling himself to his feet. "This can't be happening. It can't be. She took him. Anna took my son too."

"I don't think *she* took him," Reg offered. "I think Jeri did. Based on what we've witnessed, I think Jeri needs Mik as much as Mik needs him. I don't think the two can survive without each other."

Zachary moaned, "He can't take him. He's all I have."

A gust of wind washed over him, and he looked up and around. As he did, a stray cloud blossomed and thickened into a menacing thunderhead. Four distinct lightning bolts shot out from it. One hit where Jeri's form lay. Another struck Mik. Seconds passed, and both of them pushed up to stand.

"We have to stay here," Jeri said upon walking over to Mik. He spoke confidently, an indication that something had happened to him while he was away. To the stares of those looking on he said, "Mother has helped me understand some things better. To make it easier for me."

Zachary turned to face Mik. "You okay?"

He wobbled on his feet, but replied, "Yeah. I'm fine."

"But there were four bolts of lightning," Reg remarked. "Two are accounted for. Two aren't." They all stared toward the station house. At the front door that just opened.

"Sam?" Ghost turned to Mik. "I … I thought you said he couldn't bring him back."

"He couldn't and I don't think he did. I'm as confused as you are."

"It must've been Anna," Reg said.

"It was," a voice from behind the group said. They all spun around. "Sort of."

"Anna," Zachary gasped at the physical incarnation of his beloved wife. "Is that you? I mean—*really* you?"

Tears streamed. "It's me, Zachary. Really me."

He went to her, pulled her close then held her at arm's length. "But how?"

"My electric angel. She truly is that. She would've returned me sooner had things not happened the way they did. It was the plan all along."

Anna moved past Zachary. "You're Mik," she said as she approached her son; her eyes gleamed pride. "I'm your mother."

He smiled. "I know. I remember you. I don't know how but I do."

She turned to Jeri then, "I'm very much your mother too."

"Yes," Jeri nodded. "I know."

"I'm here to help you so you can go home someday soon. Would you like that?"

He smiled broadly and nodded. "Yes, very much."

* * *

In the thinner part of the earth's atmosphere she hovered. She couldn't take Jeri yet. He hadn't matured enough to survive without Mik's help. And she hadn't anticipated the bond between the two being so strong. She'd have to put her plan to take him home on hold. But she could wait. However long it took, she could wait.

§

Thank you so much for reading

S D Enterprise's edition of

Electric Angel

Don't hesitate to share

How much you enjoyed it.

You may visit me anytime at

www.authorsuedent.com

or

www.facebook.com/JustSueDent

For signings, personal appearances, or interviews, please
contact Ms. Dent's publicist
Matt Chassin at Mattsmarketing.com

Made in the USA
Monee, IL
06 December 2024